TEEN SPIRIT

RICHARD SLOANE

ISBN: 978-1-957956-24-4 (sc)
ISBN: 978-1-957956-25-1 (e)

Rev. date: 08/01/2022

Contents

Acknowledgements

Many thanks should go to Sam Davis at Leavitt Peak Press for editing the book so magnificently and to Mia Baker for overseeing the whole project so efficiently. This is a new edition of my book which I hope is more eye-catching and better than the previous one. It is certainly a lot more affordable for the average teenager!

Thanks too should go to my daughter, Alexia, who, when I was struggling for a word or phrase, would almost always come up with *le mot juste*. I should also apologise to her for forgetting at the last moment to dedicate my Louis Braille novel to her in the hope that this makes up for it just a little.

A nod of thanks should also go to Nirvana, whose song *Smells like Teen Spirit* gave me the idea for the title.

Chapter 1

That Friday afternoon Anna came home from school at her usual time. She opened the front door with her key and at once called out to her mother to let her know she was home as she always did. She was looking forward to spending a quiet weekend with her. But then she remembered that her mum would not be at home now. She'd told Anna that morning that she had to go out to see a prospective client in the afternoon. So she went upstairs to her room to unpack her book bag and then returned downstairs to get herself a glass of milk from the kitchen. There she noticed the answer phone was flashing so she pressed the Play button, thinking it might be her mum telling her what time she'd be back.

An impersonal voice said simply, 'This is the hospital. I have a message for Mrs Pauline Sixsmith's daughter. If she could please call us on ....' And the voice left a number.

Worried, she dialled the number and, when she got through, she said, 'This is Anna Sixsmith. I am returning your call.'

'Oh yes, Miss Sixsmith. I am very glad we managed to get hold of you. I'm afraid your mother has been in an accident. Would you be good enough to come to ward A3 as soon as you can? She asked for you.'

Her mother? She *never* had accidents! At least not ones serious enough to land her in hospital! 'I'll be right there,' she said in a panic without thinking to ask for any more details and banged down the phone. What was the quickest way to get there? A taxi was the answer. But she had almost no cash! Oh, God! Then she remembered the tin where her mother kept the loose change she didn't have room in her purse for. She checked it and to her relief found what should be enough for a taxi. She picked up the phone again and called a local taxi company. They answered almost immediately and promised they'd be there very soon. Grabbing her school jacket, she rushed out of the house and into the street where she paced frantically up and down, waiting for the taxi to arrive.

It actually came within a few minutes although it felt like a few hours to Anna. 'The hospital! As quick as you can!' she told the driver urgently. What on earth had happened to her mother? Had she been run over? Or had she had a heart attack and was even now fighting for her life? Anna was fifteen and an only child. Her parents had been divorced for years. There were only the two of them against the big, hostile world. How on earth would she cope if her mother was in a really bad way? What if Mum had to stay in hospital for quite a while? Who would take care of her? She was only a school kid after all. It was just too much to contemplate. But then she thought of her mother and how much worse *her* situation might be than her own and felt ashamed of herself for her selfish thoughts.

Fortunately, it was not far to the hospital and, when they arrived, she jumped out of the taxi, gave the driver all the money she had without waiting for change and ran inside.

Urgently Anna asked the receptionist on the main desk where ward A3 was. Following her directions, she set off at a run through the huge, unfamiliar place. She had to go up in a lift and ask the way again twice before she finally spotted the sign for A3 with an arrow pointing towards a large blue-painted swing door. It was locked and she pressed the bell outside. The intercom was answered by an anonymous female voice asking what her name was. She gave it and the door clicked open.

She went inside, into what seemed to be an atmosphere of controlled chaos. There were nurses pushing heavily bandaged people on trolleys into bays in big rooms on either side with a few empty beds in them and a number of young doctors in white coats milling around, looking rather nervous. Anna had no idea who to ask about her mother but then she noticed a woman sitting at a desk halfway down the long corridor the ward was on, clacking away on a computer. Anna approached her and she looked up and said, rather brusquely, 'What can I do for you, young lady?' Anna explained about the phone call she'd received from the hospital and gave her name again. The woman's tone changed at once and she said, 'Oh, yes. I spoke to you not long ago. Thank you for coming. Would you mind waiting in the waiting room? A doctor will be along to speak to you shortly. I'll tell him you're here.' Then she pointed up the corridor and went back to what she'd been doing.

Anna, who'd never, to the best of her recollection, been in a hospital before, was now feeling very scared indeed but she followed the woman's instructions. The waiting room seemed to be full of people talking softly but anxiously to each other and it was with some difficulty that she found an empty chair. There was a TV mounted on the wall warbling softly to itself and she noticed it seemed to be a news programme but after that she paid it no attention. She also noticed a girl of about her own age with long, dramatically red hair who was sobbing quietly into the shoulder of a man next to her. She wondered what had happened to make her cry so much. Had *her* mother also had an accident? But she knew she couldn't ask.

Finally, after an interminable wait during which Anna thought she might break down completely, an older man with perfectly groomed grey hair came in, dressed impeccably in a dark suit and dazzlingly white shirt, blue tie and highly polished black shoes. He called her name and she followed him out of the room, pursued by jealous looks from some of the people still waiting.

'We can talk in here,' he said, opening a door into a small office with a couple of chairs and a computer sitting on an otherwise empty desk. 'Well, Miss Sixsmith, the good news first,' he said, smiling after they'd sat down, 'Your mother was one of the lucky ones. She made it through the surgery although......' and here he paused, becoming more serious all of a sudden.

Anna burst out, interrupting, 'What happened to her? What do you mean 'one of the lucky ones'?'

'Hasn't anybody told you about what happened in the centre of the city this morning?'

'No. Nobody's told me anything!' Anna wailed.

'Oh, I'm so sorry. I assumed you'd been told,' the man said. Then he continued slowly, 'A bus exploded in the city centre. The police suspect terrorism. Many people lost their lives.'

Anna gasped incredulously. 'You mean my mother was travelling on a bus that got blown up?'

'No, she wasn't actually on the bus. She was apparently walking along the pavement. She just got caught up in it – in the wrong place at the wrong time, I guess. If she had been on the bus, she would almost certainly have been killed.' And here he paused again to give Anna time to assimilate this shocking information.

Anna said, 'How is she? Can I see her?'

'Not at the moment, I'm afraid. She's only just been released from intensive care after the operation. Also she's heavily bandaged. I don't think you'd even recognise her.'

'OK but how *is* she?' Anna persisted.

'She has a number of superficial injuries, lacerations from flying glass, things like that, but more seriously, I'm afraid, she has a bad head wound. She's not out of the woods yet. We're not sure how much damage it caused and it'll be a while before we find out. We'll just have to wait until she wakes up.'

'How do you know all this? Are you a doctor? You sure don't look like one,' Anna now asked rudely, realising as soon as she'd said it that she must be in shock.

'Not all doctors go around in blood-spattered white coats,' the man replied calmly, smiling again. 'I'm the surgeon who performed the operation on your mother. My name's Mr Penny. I'm sorry. I should have introduced myself earlier. It's been rather a long day.' He made this final statement while running his hands through his hair and Anna, who now looked at him closely for the first time, realised he looked tired.

'I'm sorry,' she said, blushing with embarrassment. Then

she asked irrelevantly, 'But why aren't you called Doctor Penny rather than Mr?'

'Surgeons just call themselves Mr So-and-so. It's a long tradition.'

'Sorry again. I'm so ignorant.' Anna felt the tears beginning to well up but with a huge effort she managed to control them. Then she thought of a better question. 'If my mother has a serious injury, how come she managed to ask me to come here?'

'She didn't actually *ask* you to come. The nurses told me that it was only when they looked through her ID stuff in her wallet that they found your name on the back of a passport photo of you and realised that you must be her daughter. They found your home number in the wallet too and I asked them to try to contact you but you must've been still at school.'

'Thank you,' Anna said gratefully. She'd decided that this man was kind and really had her best interests at heart. 'OK. That all makes sense.' A mistake was made. 'But when *will* I be able to see her?'

'Tomorrow, we hope.' Then he changed the subject abruptly and asked, 'How old are you, Miss Sixsmith?'

'I'm fifteen,' Anna replied with a catch in her voice.

'Oh, dear. Is your father at home? You see, I'm wondering who you can stay with until your mother gets better.'

'Oh, he left us years ago. I'm afraid there's nobody I can think of who I *could* stay with.'

'Any relatives?'

Anna shook her head. 'As far as I know, I don't have any at all who live nearby. My closest one's an uncle and he lives in America.'

'What about close friends at school maybe?'

Anna thought about her school and how she kept herself to herself, preferring the company of books to that of her classmates, which didn't exactly make her popular. She knew she could be as sociable as the next person when it came to people she respected. Unfortunately, however, she didn't actually respect the vast majority of her classmates, who she regarded as shallow and uninspiring. And she knew this feeling came across in her dealings with them. So, no, she wasn't popular but she didn't care. If this was arrogance, then so be it. She could live with it. So she just shrugged and said. 'No, I'm afraid not.'

He sighed and said, 'I'll ask around and see if I can find somebody. Would you mind waiting a bit longer?'

'Not at all. Thank you, doctor,' Anna said sincerely, adding, 'Sorry, Mr.'

The surgeon smiled and said, 'You can wait in here. At least it's quieter than the madhouse outside.'

'Thank you again, Mr Doctor. Don't be too long please. I think I might just go crazy.'

'I'll try not to be.' And he left.

Now she was alone, she let the tears flow freely, using up half a packet of tissues in the process. She knew they were mostly tears of self-pity but she didn't care. Who *could* look after her like her Mum did, doing everything from amusing her to feeding her to making sure her school uniform was clean every day? She knew she couldn't cope by herself. She was far too unworldly. Then a thought struck her. What if Mum actually died? What on earth would she do then? 'She's not going to die! I'm not going to let her!' she whispered to herself through her tears.

That made her think of all the other poor people whose relatives or friends had died that day and she suddenly forgot her own problems and started to think about theirs. She wondered momentarily if there were any other kids in her situation, like perhaps the girl with the red hair, and dried her eyes for the umpteenth time. She felt like praying to whichever God up there might be listening, something she'd almost never done before. She was not exactly an atheist but neither was she a churchgoer. When people asked, she usually said, 'I'm an agnostic,' and that seemed to satisfy them. But she managed to say a quick prayer for her mother and then just sat there, feeling totally helpless and emotionally drained. Perhaps the surgeon had forgotten all about her and her only option was to go home alone and try to look after herself? But she knew how unrealistic that was.

Finally, however, Mr Penny did return with a pleasant-looking, if slightly plump, older nurse in tow, dressed severely in a dark blue uniform. 'Sorry I've been so long,' he said. 'Miss Sixsmith, this is Mrs Frost. She's nearly finished her shift and has said she's willing to take you home with her. So I'll leave you in her capable hands, all right?' And with those words he disappeared.

Anna and Mrs Frost looked at each other warily for a moment but then the woman's kindly face broke into a big smile. 'He didn't give you much choice in the matter, did he? Typical surgeon! What's your name, by the way? I can't keep calling you Miss Sixsmith!' she said.

Anna tried to smile back. 'Anna,' she said, adding, 'Did he give you any?'

'Oh, don't worry about me, Anna. I've always wanted to have a girl around the house. First question though: Where do you live?' Anna gave her the name of her street and the house number. The woman clapped her hands together almost girlishly and exclaimed, 'That's only a few streets away from me! I'll drop by there before we go home so you can pick up the things you need.'

'Thanks, Mrs Frost,' Anna said sincerely.

'Do please call me Gemma. Mrs Frost sounds so formal.'

'OK....Gemma,' Anna replied hesitantly. She already liked this lady and was surprised at how other people could suddenly take over her life like this. 'Do you have a family?' she asked politely, not really caring as she still felt completely wretched.

'A husband who, to be honest, is pretty useless and a son who I guess must be about your age.'

'I'm fifteen.'

'Graham's sixteen going on sixty.'

'What *do* you mean?'

'Oh, he almost never goes out to have fun. He seems to be quite content to curl up with a book or his computer at home.'

'Sounds just my type,' Anna said, managing a small rueful grin.

Gemma grinned back and said, 'I've got a couple of quick things to do and then I'll be back.'

'That's fine. I'll be OK. Can I stay in here?'

'Yes, I don't see why not. None of the doctors appear to need this room at present. See you soon then.'

And she left Anna alone with her thoughts. She was still feeling distraught but she was slightly happier about her own future now that it'd been taken out of her hands. Then she thought how much she wanted to catch even a glimpse of her mother and she came to a sudden decision. As her mum was nearby, there was no reason why she shouldn't go looking for her. She had noticed when she came into the ward that most of the individual rooms had medical charts outside them in little boxes with the patient's name printed clearly at the top. She knew she wouldn't be allowed in any of the large rooms, which had many beds and big signs outside saying Bay 1, 2 or 3 and so on, but she reckoned that her mother would be in an individual room.

So she cautiously opened the door and peered out. Nobody seemed remotely interested in her. They were all much too busy. If stopped, she could always say she was looking for a toilet. She squared her shoulders and, trying not to look like a criminal, walked brazenly down the long corridor towards the opposite end from which she'd entered the ward. She noticed as she passed the waiting room that the girl with red hair was no longer there. The further she walked, the more signs on the doors she noticed saying 'Barrier Nursing' in big red letters. Underneath there was a list of things you had to do before you could enter, including scrubbing your hands and wearing a mask and gown. But there were small windows in each door and she only wanted to take a quick peek.

Suddenly off on the left she spotted her mother's name, Mrs P. Sixsmith, and with much trepidation she approached the door. It also had the words 'Barrier Nursing' on it. But, looking through the little window, she was disappointed to see only a view of dark blue curtains, obviously surrounding a bed. Then she spotted her mother's handbag on a nightstand just outside the curtains and knew she must have the right room.

She couldn't stay there long; somebody was bound to ask what she wanted. But then a pair of feet emerged from under the curtains and suddenly they were pulled back. A nurse appeared but she didn't look up. She was too busy fiddling with one of the complicated-looking machines beside the bed. But who or what was that in the bed? It couldn't be her mum, could it? It looked like an Egyptian mummy. Swathes of white bandages covering the top of the head. A plastic mask over the nose and mouth. A blue blanket covering the rest of the body. For a split second Anna was sure they must be treating the wrong person. But no, it must be her mum. She knew that from the handbag. And she was in a bad way, much worse than Anna had imagined.

What exactly had the surgeon said? 'You probably won't even recognise her' and 'She has a serious head wound. We won't know how she is until she wakes up.' Or words to that effect. Anna realised at once that her mother must be in a coma. She knew, from watching occasional hospital dramas on TV, as much about comas as the average layperson – that, for example, sometimes they *never* woke up and in the end, with the permission of the family, the life support machines were switched off. Also that, even if they *did* wake up, they could have serious problems with their memories or their power of speech. Was that what she had to look forward to?

With these grim thoughts swirling around her brain, she knew it was time to leave and with a last, desperately sad look through the window, she started back down the corridor.

<h1 style="text-align:center">Chapter 2</h1>

As Anna walked back to the small office, she knew she would have to be strong, if only for her mother's sake, and promised herself no more tears, at least for the present. Then she saw Gemma come out of another patient's side room. She waved and hurried up to her.

'Can we get out of this place now?' she asked.

'Sure,' Gemma replied. 'I know how intimidating it can be if you're not familiar with it. Let me just collect my things.' And she disappeared into a small room with a large number of lockers in it. She came out very quickly, carrying a handbag and a shopping bag, and walked beside Anna to the entrance of the hospital. Anna didn't want to talk yet and Gemma respected this, not asking her anything.

When they got outside, Anna took a deep lungful of fresh air and said, 'That's better. It's too warm in there.'

Gemma smiled and said, 'I know. It can be very stifling at times, even if you're used to it. But it needs to be warm for the patients. Follow me. The car's not far away.'

They got to the huge car park and Anna climbed into the front seat of Gemma's small car. As they left the hospital, Anna suddenly remembered that she had no money at all. She had spent everything she had on the taxi and the house, as far as she knew, was now empty of cash. Could she ask Gemma for some? Fortunately, she had her school bus pass, which enabled her to get to school without paying but she wasn't even sure if she'd be going back to school in the near future. That was something else she needed to do. Ring them to tell them what'd happened. All these responsibilities on top of her deep worry about her mum!

She decided she couldn't be coy about this issue of money and had to come straight out with it. So she asked Gemma if it might be possible to borrow some, promising to pay it back as soon as she could. Gemma looked away from the road a second, smiled and said, 'Of course you can, Anna. You shouldn't have to be worrying about money at a time like this. Peter will lend you whatever you need. Don't worry.'

'Thank you. Who's Peter?' Anna said.

'My husband. I said before that he was useless but I was only joking. There are some things he's very good at and one of them is making money.'

Anna had a momentary vision of staying with a bank robber or a major fraudster but put it aside and asked, 'Oh, what does he do?'

'He runs his own business, programming the computers of banks. Don't ask me what it involves. I haven't the faintest idea.'

Banks wouldn't entrust their computers to a crook, Anna thought with relief. Then they arrived in her street and Anna pointed out her house. It was a normal, small terraced house which looked pretty much identical to all the others in the row except that hers had a brightly painted, purple front door. Gemma parked outside and Anna invited her in, taking her key from her jacket pocket. At least she had remembered *that* in her panic to leave! They went in and down a small hallway to the living room on the right. Gemma stepped inside and said, 'Why, this is lovely.'

'We like it,' Anna said proudly. 'Mum's an interior designer and she did it all herself.' Gemma was wandering around, looking at the modern art prints on the clean, white walls and pale woollen rug on the light, hardwood floor. There were a number of photos scattered around, mainly of Anna and her Mum on holiday in England, and Gemma looked at them curiously.

'I know it's none of my business,' she said, 'but there are no photos of men. I presume your father doesn't live here with you. This is a very feminine room.'

'You're right. He doesn't. He and Mum got divorced years ago and since then it's just been Mum and me.'

'Oh, I wondered why Mr Penny had asked me to take you home. I assumed wrongly that maybe your Dad was an invalid or in hospital himself or something. He should have told me more about you but, like all surgeons, he probably thought it wasn't important.' And she smiled wryly.

'Yes, I have nowhere at all to go – no relatives, no close friends. As I said, it's just Mum and me.' And her words made her want to cry again.

'You poor child,' Gemma murmured.

Anna pulled herself together and said stiffly and rather ungratefully, she realised immediately, 'It's worked fine until now.'

Gemma gave her a pitying look but then said practically, 'You run along and collect your stuff. I'll phone Peter to let him know we're both on the way. He doesn't know about you yet.'

'I hope he's OK with a complete stranger invading his house,' Anna said.

'Oh, he'll be fine. I know he'll like you.'

Anna was worried about this additional complication but ran upstairs to her bedroom anyway without another word. She piled a few clothes and books on her bed and then looked in the mirror on the back of her bedroom door. She was shocked by how pale she looked and how her teenage acne stood out even more against the paleness. But she had worse things to worry about than acne. Then she packed her laptop away in its case and got her toiletries out of the bathroom, hurriedly washing her tear-streaked face while she was there. Finally, she went into her mother's bedroom and from inside her big wardrobe took the large suitcase they used for travelling. Carrying it back to her own bedroom, she hastily packed everything away in it and lugged it with difficulty downstairs. There she found Gemma putting her mobile phone back in her handbag.

'I've spoken to Peter and, as I said, he's fine with it. Do you have everything you need?' Gemma said.

'I think so,' Anna replied.

'Good. Let's go then, shall we?'

As they went outside, Anna noticed that the warm, late spring sun was starting to set and she wondered where the day had gone. A few hours ago she'd been in school as usual and now her whole life had been turned upside down. But she knew she just had to go along with everything that was happening to her, however upsetting it all was. They put the heavy suitcase on the back seat after Anna had locked the front door. She looked wistfully back at the house for a moment and Gemma must have caught the look for she turned to Anna before she started the engine and said seriously, 'I know how disruptive all this must be for you.' Then she added smiling, 'Look on it as an adventure.'

'I'll try,' said Anna, grateful for the sympathy but almost on the point of tears again. Then they were off to her new home.

Chapter 3

On the way Gemma asked Anna a few questions about herself without being too intrusive and Anna was grateful to have her mind taken off her awful predicament and for being treated like an adult. But they were very soon there and Gemma pulled into the driveway of a detached house which looked to Anna like a rather imposing mansion.

'Wow!' she said, impressed. 'Do you live here?'

'Yes. I told you Peter has a knack for making money, didn't I?' Gemma said but she didn't wait for a reply, getting out of the car and heading straight for the house. Then a big, burly man with longish salt and pepper hair and a well-maintained beard came out through the front door, said 'Hi, darling!' and enveloped her in a big hug. She responded by giving him a kiss on the cheek and the big man came up to Anna, who had only just got out of the car, held out his hand and boomed, 'Hi, I'm Peter. You must be Anna. Welcome to our humble abode.'

Anna shook his hand meekly, wondering if hers was going to be crushed although, in fact, his touch was gentle. He took her suitcase out of the car as if it weighed nothing at all and went back into the house, calling back over his shoulder, 'Don't just stand there, girls. Come on in.' Anna found him overwhelming but lovely at the same time, rather like a giant teddy bear, and glanced at Gemma.

She grinned and said as they walked to the house, 'Yes, I know. He is a bit larger than life, isn't he? But you'll soon get used to him. It's rather like having a St Bernard around.' And Anna managed to give her a genuine grin back this time, glad of her understanding and her sense of humour.

She followed Gemma into the big hallway of the house and looked around curiously. It was very untidy, that was for sure. There were shoes and boots lying all over the floor and, when Anna looked through an open doorway, all she could see was piles of books and papers littering the floor of what was probably Peter's office. Gemma had told her he ran his own business so he must work from home like her mother. Actually she was rather glad the place wasn't immaculate as that might have been too intimidating. The untidiness gave the house a homely feel and she already felt as if she might be able to fit in here.

'Sorry about the mess,' Peter said, dumping her suitcase on what looked like an old oak chest off to one side of the hallway and adding, 'I was working and saw you guys arriving through the office window. Come on upstairs, Anna, and I'll show you your room. Don't worry, Gemma, I've tidied everything up in there.'

'You've what?' Gemma said in a disbelieving tone, obviously teasing him.

'Don't believe me? Come and see for yourself.'

So they all trooped up a wide staircase, Peter carrying Anna's suitcase in one hand, and went down a corridor to the very end. Anna noticed there were about six doors leading off it but they were all shut. Then Peter opened a door on the right, saying 'Et voila!' as he went inside. When Anna entered, she gasped and said, 'Can I really stay in here?'

It was a large room with a dark blue carpet, an unmade double bed, a nice desk and chair and a few other bits and pieces of decent furniture. She could also see it had an en suite bathroom off to one side which had the door open. But what she liked most about it was the huge picture window taking up almost the whole of one wall, which looked out over a large, well-tended garden with trees, shrubs and flower beds as well as an immaculately cropped lawn.

'I hope you like it,' Peter said, sounding anxious.

'Like it? I absolutely love it,' Anna gushed.

Gemma asked, 'What did you do with the stuff that was in here?'

'Shoved it in the small, spare bedroom,' Peter said. 'Sorry I didn't make the bed or put clean towels in the bathroom but I'm not sure where they're kept.'

Gemma rolled her eyes at Anna saying, 'What did I tell you? Completely useless!' but she smiled at her husband as she said it, taking the sting out of the comment.

'It's nearly suppertime,' Peter said, ignoring Gemma's words, 'and I don't know about you two but I'm starving.'

'You'd starve to death without me. You do know that, Peter, don't you?'

'Yes, darling, I do,' Peter replied, smacking her bottom lightly and smiling at her. Anna could feel the love between them and it cheered her up a bit.

'I'll bring you a couple of towels so you can get washed if you want and we'll make the bed later but we'll leave you to get unpacked now, OK?' Gemma said, adding, 'Supper should be on the table in about half an hour. Come downstairs when you're ready.'

'Thank you, Gemma,' Anna said weakly. 'You're doing too much for me.'

'Nonsense, girl. I just hope somebody does the same for me when I need it,' Gemma replied, leaving the room with her husband.

Anna sat down heavily on the bed and Gemma reappeared almost instantly with the towels. She unpacked quickly, putting her clothes away neatly in the big chest of drawers or hanging them in the vast in-built wardrobe and putting her books and laptop on the desk. Then she decided she needed a shower and a change of clothes. She didn't want to appear for dinner in her school uniform and, as it was a Friday, she wouldn't need it until at least Monday – if she went back to school then. So she went into her very own bathroom - something she'd never had before - and had a quick shower, washing her long, blonde hair and drying it with the hair dryer she found there. Finally she put on her favourite jeans and blouse and combed her hair, checking her appearance in the big mirror on the wardrobe door. There was little evidence to show of her former tears although her face was still very pale. Just about presentable but it's still a pity about the spots, she thought.

She opened the door of her room and peered out. The upper floor of the house seemed empty – at least all the doors were shut and there was no noise coming from any of the other rooms - but she could hear sounds coming from what must be the kitchen below. So she walked along the corridor and downstairs in their direction. She peeked in a few rooms on the way, noticing a smallish living room and what seemed to be a large games room, before arriving at the back of the house where the sounds seemed to originate.

It was a big, airy kitchen with a large, scrubbed wooden table in the middle and another door leading out to the garden. Peter was laying the table and Gemma was busy with pots and pans.

'Good timing,' Peter said, looking up. 'Supper's nearly ready. You look different now you're not in your school uniform.'

'I hope I look OK,' Anna said, blushing at what she hoped was a compliment.

Gemma turned around now and said, 'You look lovely, my dear,' and Anna was reassured by her words. Then she added, 'When you've done that, Peter, can you call that lazy son of ours to the table.'

Graham! She'd completely forgotten about him! She hoped fervently she was going to get along with him and that he wasn't going to resent her being around. She didn't like most of the boys she knew, thinking that they were either idiots or hopeless or usually both, and she prayed that Graham would be different. She offered to help Peter with the table and they quickly finished the job. Then Peter went out of the kitchen to the foot of the stairs and his booming voice could be heard calling Graham to eat.

'Coming!' a light boy's voice replied and she heard a clattering of feet on the stairs.

CHAPTER 4

Anna was putting the full soup bowls on the table when Graham came in so she didn't see him immediately. But, when she looked up, she saw a strikingly good-looking boy. He was tall and lanky with very pale almost translucent skin and short dark hair. Then she noticed his eyes. They were a deep brown, brimming with curiosity and intelligence and, at the moment, they were wide open, staring at her in amazement.

'Who on earth are *you*?' he demanded in a cut-glass, posh BBC kind of voice.

As soon as she heard this, Anna knew instinctively that she'd have to talk properly to him like she did to her teachers so that he'd have no excuse to laugh at her for her normal inner-city accent. 'My name's Anna. I've come to stay for a while,' she said equably but thinking 'Oh, no! An upper-class git! Great!'

'Oh, I'm sorry. I was so busy I completely forgot to tell you she was coming,' Peter said from one end of the table.

'Oh! Peter!' Gemma said in exasperation, sitting down at the other end. Graham sat opposite Anna and he continued staring at her until she looked down, blushing, and started to have her soup.

'*Why* is she here?' Graham now demanded of his parents.

Gemma replied for her, saying simply, 'Her mother's in hospital and she didn't have anywhere to go so I invited her to stay. I'm sure Anna will add more details if you ask her nicely.'

He had the goodness to blush at her sharp words and apologised to Anna, saying, 'I'm sorry, Anna. It was a bit of a shock, that's all. My parents don't usually invite strange girls to the house.'

Anna was determined not to be put off by his former rudeness or his obvious poshness and she shot back, glaring at him, 'I'm not that strange, am I?' Then he smiled at her, the smile lighting up his whole face. Her heart, which had been sinking at his earlier words, now seemed to beat faster. 'I do hope we're going to get on,' she now added slowly although she rather doubted it.

'Oh, I think there's a reasonable chance of that,' he said, grinning through a mouthful of soup.

'Good,' Gemma interrupted now. 'By the way, Anna, I forgot to ask if you were a vegetarian or had any special food allergies.'

'No to both questions. I like just about everything,' Anna replied, tearing her eyes away from Graham to his mother.

'Good. That's a relief. If you have anything you especially like, do tell me, won't you?'

Anna promised she would and quickly finished her soup without looking at Graham again. 'That was lovely,' she said and Gemma acknowledged the compliment by smiling at her.

'Yes, she's a good cook, Gemma is. That's why I married her,' Peter said, teasing his wife.

Gemma said nothing but cleared away the bowls and

Graham sat back in his chair, looking directly at Anna without a trace of animosity now. 'Tell me about yourself, Anna,' he said.

'What do you want to know?'

'Well, where do you go to school for a start?'

'To the local comprehensive. And you?'

'Oh, you're lucky. I go to St Paul's. It's all boys so I don't often get to meet girls.'

Anna knew of St Paul's. It was an expensive, private school not far away but she refused to be intimidated by this. She realised at once that the school must be the reason for his accent as neither of his parents had a similar one so he couldn't really be blamed for it. 'Well, now you've met one,' she said and she managed to smile at him. He beamed back at her and she realised she might, after all, be able to actually like this boy.

'What's the matter with your mum?' he asked now.

'She was involved in a bomb incident and now she's in some kind of coma, I think,' she replied, glancing at Gemma for support. But Graham's parents had clearly decided to let them get on with the conversation by themselves and they didn't say anything.

'Oh, that's terrible,' he said sympathetically. 'I heard about the bombing at school today.' But he didn't say any more as his mother had brought the main course, a large dish of lasagne, and, when he was served, he started hoovering up the food as if he hadn't eaten for months. Anna thought irrelevantly that it must cost quite a bit to feed his tall, slim body.

No more words were exchanged while they were all eating and when they'd finished and cleared away the dirty plates,

Gemma brought the dessert, a large bowl of homemade ice cream each. Anna hadn't felt hungry when they'd started. She'd wondered whether it was the shock of what had happened as she normally had a good appetite but when she was actually presented with the food, she devoured everything quickly. Then she sat back, realising suddenly how tired she was. That day she'd been through more than she'd ever had to go through before, more indeed than anybody *should* have to, but she hoped that a reasonable night's sleep would refresh her at least a little. She offered to help the adults clear up but Gemma told her it wouldn't take a moment and shooed her and Graham out of the kitchen. She called out to Anna as she was leaving that she'd do the bed as soon as she'd finished tidying up. Anna called back thanking her and she and Graham walked together up the stairs.

'Would you like to see my room?' Graham asked her shyly.

'Just for a moment,' she said, feeling apprehensive about this invitation. 'I'm really tired and need to go to bed.'

'That's fine,' he said and opened one of the doors on the corridor upstairs. 'You'll be the first girl I've ever invited in here.'

'I'm honoured,' she said as he went in, Anna following him.

The room seemed to be at first glance in total chaos with his school clothes slung carelessly everywhere, bits of what looked like a computer being built lying all over the floor and a large model train set in one corner.

'Sorry about the mess,' he said, echoing his father's words when she'd first entered the house. He hastily picked up some of the clothes and stuffed them into a large wardrobe. She presumed he took after his father in his disdain for tidiness.

Looking curiously around, she could see no posters of rock stars on the walls, just one of an ancient-looking guy playing a trumpet and another of a French film she'd never heard of.

She went over to his CD collection which was housed on shelves above the desk on which his laptop sat. She liked music and was interested in his tastes. But, unlike every other teenager she knew, there wasn't a single one of any contemporary group she'd heard of, just a lot of classical music and jazz. This interested her and she asked him about it. He told her that Peter had been a jazz musician in his younger days and that he'd been influenced greatly by Peter's tastes in music. This made good sense and she found it fascinating that Peter had once been a jazz musician. She resolved to ask him about it when he was free.

Then she looked at his books, which were in a bookcase along one wall and were her main passion in life. There was lots of sci-fi and fantasy along with classic fiction and quite a few books on computers and how to programme them.

'You like sci-fi, I see. So do I,' she said.

'Who's your favourite writer?' he asked eagerly.

'Oh, I have lots. Robert Sheckley, Philip K. Dick, Isaac Asimov, Ray Bradbury, and John Wyndham among others.'

He looked impressed but then they were interrupted by a knock on the door. It was Gemma to say that she'd made the bed. Anna thanked her and turned to Graham, 'I really am tired, Graham. I'll see you tomorrow, OK?'

'Yes, fine,' he said although Anna could have sworn he looked disappointed, which somehow pleased her.

Gemma said, 'Get up whenever you like. I'm not working

this weekend and can take you back to the hospital if you wish.'

Her mother! How could she have forgotten her so quickly? She knew it was all because of Graham and felt ashamed of herself and her wretched hormones. 'Thanks again, Gemma,' she said and left Graham's room, walking slowly back to her own. She did all the usual things she did before she went to bed and then curled up under the warm duvet. She could hear what she presumed was the faint sound of the TV coming from downstairs and that of the house settling down for the night. There was no traffic noise at all here at the back of the big house and she found this rather disconcerting at first, having lived with its background drone all her life.

She thought about her mother and about how she'd cope in the long term without her and that nearly reduced her to tears again. But she reminded herself that she had to be strong and not too pessimistic. With these thoughts in her mind she drifted slowly off to sleep and, feeling perfectly safe in her new bed, slept better than she had expected except for waking up in the middle of the night with a nightmare. However, she managed to go back to sleep again quite soon and, when she woke up the next morning, she'd forgotten the details of the nightmare. Even though she still felt wretched inside, she did indeed feel more refreshed and less brittle than she'd have thought possible the day before.

CHAPTER 5

Anna looked in her bathroom mirror and saw that, although she was still very pale, she had a little more colour in her cheeks than the day before. She went downstairs, meeting up with the family in the kitchen who were eating breakfast and listening to the news on the radio. Gemma, however, tactfully switched it off as soon as Anna came in. However, she just caught the tail-end of a report about the bombing of the day before and started to feel distressed all over again.

'How did you sleep?' Peter asked.

'Better than I'd have thought possible under the circumstances. I must've been exhausted last night,' she replied.

Graham fixed her with one of his penetrating looks but she ignored him and sat down. After breakfast Gemma asked her if she wanted to return to the hospital and she said uncertainly, 'Yes, I suppose I should,' not really wanting to go back inside that unfamiliar, sterile environment and see her mother in the state she'd seen her in the day before.

'I'll come with you if you want,' Graham said, almost the first words he'd spoken since she'd appeared for breakfast, and she felt a strange rush of affection for him and his thoughtfulness.

'If you really don't mind, I'd like that,' she replied.

So the decision was made and, after the dishes had been cleared away, the three of them piled into Gemma's car and Peter waved them off as they left. When they arrived at the hospital, Gemma led the way up to the ward and Anna peeked in through the window of her mother's room. She saw that her head bandage was still in place and she lay there under the blankets like a waxen image with her mask on, unmoving and wired up to the battery of machines she had caught a glimpse of the day before. She looked so small and frail, Anna thought sadly.

Then Gemma came back from her conversation with the ward sister on duty and told her and Graham she'd said they could stay as long as they liked but they had to comply with the rules of Barrier Nursing. She added that she had to run a few errands but would return after a couple of hours. So, after they'd washed their hands with a kind of special soap and put on gowns and masks, which they agreed felt very strange, Anna tentatively entered her mother's room. She sat in a chair on one side of her bed while Graham took one on the other side. She grasped her mother's cold hand fiercely and whispered, 'Hello, Mum. It's me, Anna,' but there was no response. This disappointed her until she remembered what Mr Penny had said about just having to wait until she woke up. Then she looked up at Graham and introduced him saying, 'Mum, this is Graham. I'm staying in his house until you get better. His mum's a nurse here and his dad has his own company. They live in a nice house and are looking after me very well. So please don't worry about me.'

She chattered on inconsequentially for a bit, telling her about her room and its lovely view as well as the fact that she had her own bathroom. But she soon ran out of words and, when there was still no response, she thought she might burst into tears. However, she managed to fight them back and gripped her mother's hand still more tightly. Then she looked up, catching a look of sympathy on Graham's face, and was glad he was there with her. But she hoped she wouldn't cry in front of him.

Shortly afterwards a nurse came in and smiled brightly at her. 'You must be the daughter,' she said. 'The more you talk to her, the better.' Then she started fiddling with the machines and taking her Mum's blood pressure and temperature and Anna asked, 'When do you think she'll wake up?'

The nurse looked sadly at her and replied, 'I'm afraid nobody knows that. But all her vital signs are good.' She paused and then said, 'Mr Penny should be in shortly to examine her. You should ask *him* your questions really.' And she left, having added to the list of medical notes hanging at the end of her bed.

Graham now spoke up for the first time. 'I guess Mr Penny's her consultant. Right?'

'Yes, I suppose he is,' Anna replied sadly. 'He's the one who operated on her. He asked your mother to take me in.'

'Well, I'm jolly glad he did,' he said with a smile and Anna managed a small smile back at him, saying, 'So am I.'

That seemed to break the ice between them and they started chatting. Anna asked him if he'd ever been in hospital and he told her that he'd had to go in a couple of times when he was very young, first for an operation to remove his tonsils and adenoids and soon afterwards for a haemorrhage, caused by the first operation. He added that he remembered very clearly how scared he'd been although he'd been excited too by all the attention he was shown. Next they exchanged some information about their schools and their favourite subjects – English for Anna and IT for Graham. After that they talked about the books they liked and Anna admitted that she was an omnivorous reader, not very particular in her tastes.

'What do you want to be when you grow up?' Graham asked then.

'Maybe a librarian,' she replied. 'And you?'

'I'm not sure yet either. But it will probably be something to do with computers. I seem to have inherited my Dad's interest in them.' Remembering the bits of what had looked like a computer on his bedroom floor, she asked him about them and he told her he was trying to build his own.

Their conversation was interrupted by the arrival of Mr Penny with three young doctors in tow. He looked at Anna and asked how it was going at Mrs Frost's.

'Fine, thanks,' she replied. 'This is Graham, her son.'

'Nice to meet you, young man,' he said, proffering his hand. Graham shook it and the surgeon said, 'Would you two mind waiting outside while we conduct our examination? I'll have a word with you when I finish.'

So they left the room and leaned against the wall outside. Graham turned to Anna and said with a grin, 'Not a man to waste words, is he?' and Anna agreed distractedly. They stood in silence for a while until Mr Penny came out. He told the trio of young doctors to wait for him outside and led the two of them back into Anna's mother's room. Then he turned to Anna and said simply, 'Questions?'

'I want to know how she is and what her chances of recovery are,' she replied.

'Well, physically your mother seems to be making a good recovery from all her superficial wounds and her brain scans show relatively normal. However, the head is a very complex thing. We still don't understand it fully. We know she's sustained a major trauma to the left side of her brain. But people have recovered fully from worse. How long it will take her to wake up is anybody's guess. And, as I told you yesterday, we'll have to wait for that to happen before we can tell whether any permanent damage has been done. OK?'

'She's not going to die, is she?' Anna burst out.

'That's very unlikely. We will keep feeding her intravenously and on the life support machines for as long as it takes.'

'Thank you, Doctor,' Anna whispered, almost in tears again as she was not totally reassured by his words.

'You can certainly help her by being at her bedside and talking to her. The sound of your voice may reawaken her. It's certainly happened in the past. Leave your mobile number with the nursing staff and we'll notify you as soon as there is any change in her condition. She's in good hands here. Try not to worry.'

'Thank you again, Doctor,' Anna said. But the surgeon had already left the room.

They sat down again and Graham said quietly, 'I can't imagine what you must be going through. If my parents were in a similar condition, I probably would have torn out all my hair by now.' Anna smiled wanly at him without replying. Then she glanced at her watch and saw that it was almost 12 o'clock. Where had the morning gone? She held her mother's hand tightly, saying in her head over and over again to her mum, 'You are going to get better. You are going to get better,' like a mantra.

Then Gemma reappeared in the room and said, 'Well, I've done everything I needed to do. Let's go home and have some lunch. You've got to eat, Anna, to keep your strength up.' And reluctantly she let go of her mother's hand and followed Gemma and Graham out of the room. However, before leaving the hospital, she remembered to give her mobile number to the nurse at the desk and was promised that they'd ring if there was any change.

<h1 style="text-align:center">Chapter 6</h1>

When they got back to the house, Gemma sent Graham upstairs and then pulled an envelope from her handbag, handing it to Anna. She peeked inside. It seemed to be full of bank notes. 'I took it out of the bank this morning for you, Anna. It should keep you going for a while.'

'But I can't accept all this!' Anna cried, feeling tears of gratitude pricking her eyes.

'You certainly can and you will,' Gemma said. 'It's Peter's money and he offered it willingly.'

Gratefully Anna said, 'I promise I'll pay him back.'

'You can pay him back by coming and giving *me* a hand in the kitchen,' Gemma replied smiling.

Anna smiled back at her and thought how lucky she had been to find such a kind family to take her in.

So they went through to the kitchen and Anna helped prepare lunch. She found the activity soothing and it helped to take her mind off her mother. Gemma asked if she would like to listen to the 1 o'clock news on the radio and Anna hesitated for a moment, unsure how she would react to stories about the bombing. But then she realised she couldn't put her head in the sand for ever. Reality would have to intrude some time and it might as well be now. So she nodded her agreement.

The first news report was about how the police were still hunting any remaining terrorists as they did not believe that the suicide bomber on the bus had been acting alone. Anna fervently hoped that they caught them soon, put them away for good and threw away the keys. At first she was surprised at this visceral anger but then accepted it as natural. She was sure that the families of the other victims would feel exactly the same way. There was also speculation as to the intended target as the bomb seemed to have gone off accidentally since there were no obvious targets on the bus. They were all, apparently, innocent victims. The news reader, however, did admit that completely random acts of violence seemed to be becoming more common. The next report was about the upcoming funerals of the victims, not all of whom had been identified yet. However, many of them were to be buried privately the following Saturday after a big memorial service at the cathedral in the city, once their bodies had been released from the mortuary.

Anna turned to Gemma and said simply, 'I'd like to go to the memorial service.'

Gemma just nodded and said, 'If you're sure, I'll take you.' Once again Anna was grateful for her understanding. Then she asked Anna to call Peter and Graham to the table. So she ran upstairs and knocked on Graham's door. When she was told to enter, she went in and found him lying on his bed staring at the ceiling. 'Lunch time,' she said and went to find Peter. He was in his messy office, looking at a long roll of computer printout with a bunch of, to Anna's eyes, meaningless mathematical squiggles on it. First she thanked him for the money but he just shrugged off her thanks, saying it was the least he could do. Then she gave him the message about lunch and he said, 'Give me a couple of minutes.'

She went back to the kitchen and found Graham already there, sitting at the table. She told Gemma what Peter had said and Gemma rolled her eyes, saying, 'Well, we might as well start. There's no point in waiting for him. He could be hours.'

So the three of them started eating. But then Graham looked up from his plate and said, 'I usually go swimming on a Saturday afternoon. How do you fancy coming with me, Anna?'

Anna hadn't discussed favourite sports with him but it just so happened that swimming was what she was best at and she loved it. She liked the fact that it was an individual sport, pitting just herself against somebody else. She thought about the idea and tried to decide if she should go back to the hospital or take her mind off it completely. Then she remembered that the ward had her mobile number so she could take her phone with her and leave it switched on. All these thoughts flashed through her mind in an instant. 'There's only one problem,' she said. 'I haven't got my swimming costume with me.'

Gemma broke in saying, 'Oh, that's not a problem. You can go back to your house to get it with Graham and can borrow my bike if you like. You could keep it to travel around. I rarely use it. Graham goes everywhere on his bike anyway.'

Anna felt overwhelmed once more by her generosity but said only, 'Thank you very much, Gemma. I haven't ridden a bike since I was at primary school. My mother always thought the city was too unsafe for me to travel around on one by myself so I've always taken buses. But I'm sure, with Graham's help, I'll be fine.'

'OK. That's settled then,' Gemma said and they finished eating. Just as they were about to clear away the plates, Peter came in and said apologetically, 'Terribly sorry, Gemma. Got a bit held up. Any chance of some grub?'

Gemma waved her hand at the pots on the stove and said, 'It's still warm. Help yourself. The kids are about to go swimming and I have my aerobics class.'

'OK, thanks,' Peter said. 'Have fun, kids. See you later, sweetheart. I'll clear up in here.'

Gemma went up to him and gave him a peck on the cheek in response. Then she led Graham and Anna out of the front door and round to the big garage which stood next to the house. She unlocked the door and pushed it up to reveal an astonishing array of cardboard boxes which seemed to fill it almost from floor to ceiling. 'This is all Peter's old computer stuff which he can't bear to part with. I've threatened many a time to take the lot to a car boot sale and flog it off for whatever I can get but I haven't got around to it – yet.' Then she pulled out from the side what looked like a brand-new lady's mountain bike and presented it to Anna with a flourish. 'Graham can adjust the saddle if it needs it,' she said. Then she added, feeling the tyres. 'The tyre pressures seem fine. It was serviced not long ago. Look after her, won't you, Graham?'

'Yes, Mum. Don't worry. You run along to your class. We'll be OK,' he replied. And she left them, climbing into her car and driving off.

Graham and Anna were alone now, almost for the first time since they'd met. Anna didn't really count that morning when they'd sat with her mother's apparently lifeless form between them but when she'd somehow still seemed present or the brief time in his bedroom the evening before. They looked at each other but Graham just said practically, 'Why don't you practise a bit around here?' So Anna got gingerly onto the bike and set off around the big front garden, wobbling a bit at first but rapidly gaining in confidence. When she felt thoroughly safe, she came up to where Graham was standing watching her and braked gently to a stop.

'It's true what they say,' she said in some amazement. 'Once you've learned to ride a bike, you never really forget.'

'Good', replied Graham with a beam of pleasure. 'I've got to go back into the house to get my swimming stuff. Is there anything you need?'

'No, I don't think so,' she replied but then smacked her forehead. 'Stupid me! I need the front door key of the house and my mobile,' and they walked back inside together.

'Won't be a mo,' Graham said, heading towards his room.

'Same,' Anna replied, slipping back briefly into the teenage language all her peers at school used. She headed off to her own room where she picked up her school rucksack and her mobile, made sure she had her key and ran back outside. It was a fine day, she thought, looking up at the sky. Nice weather for a cycle ride. Graham reappeared quickly, carrying a rucksack of his own, and went round to the back of the house where he collected his own bike from a shed.

They set off after Anna had told him the name of her street. 'Oh, yes. I know it,' he said. 'I often cycle down it.

Keep behind me all the time,' and she promised she would. She had no intention of trying to overtake him and risking her life in the busy city traffic, in spite of all the cycle lanes the council had put in over the past few years.

They soon got safely to her street and Anna invited him into the house. He came in behind her and said, much like his mother had done, 'Wow! This is cool!' She explained again about her Mum being an interior designer and then went upstairs to get her swimming stuff. When she came down, she found him looking at the photos in the living room, also like his mother had done.

'You were a cute kid, weren't you?' he said.

'So I've been told,' Anna replied. 'Pity it didn't last.'

Graham smiled and said, 'I don't think there's much wrong with your looks.'

Anna blushed and said, 'Thanks but don't talk rubbish. Let's go, shall we?'

They left her house and set off for the swimming pool but Anna soon realised that they were going the wrong way for the local council pool. She called out from her position behind, 'Where are we going?'

'We're going to my school. I always swim there. Sorry, I forgot to tell you,' Graham called back.

'Oh, I thought I was being kidnapped,' Anna said.

Graham slowed, turned round for a second, beamed and said in a mock American accent, 'In your dreams, baby.' Anna laughed so much she nearly fell off the bike. She had thought she might never laugh properly again and was grateful to him for taking her mind off her mother's plight, however briefly.

Chapter 7

It was some way to Graham's school but he knew all the shortcuts and it didn't take them long to get there. When they arrived at the massive gateway, Graham braked and Anna pulled up beside him. 'Wow!' she said. 'This is impressive!'

'I suppose it is if you don't have to go to school here,' Graham answered, adding, 'but at least it has a decent-sized indoor pool which isn't too crowded.'

'Do you have any girls here?' Anna asked, curious to know.

'In the past few years a few girls have been allowed into the 6th form,' he replied.

'So at least you have girls changing rooms?'

'Yeah, sure.'

'Thank God for that.'

When he heard that, Graham gave her a wicked, little grin. 'I'll give you a quick tour later if you'd like,' he said.

'Yes, I'd be very interested to see the inner workings of a real live public school,' she replied sarcastically but truthfully.

Then, wheeling their bikes, he took her through a door in the gateway where Anna was confronted by a huge courtyard and opposite what looked to her like a massive castle made of old, red brick with many outbuildings, obviously added on much later. They went around the back of the main school past enormous playing fields, which must have been ten times larger than those at her comprehensive, and finally into another big, modern building. It smelled of chlorine and Anna knew this must be the swimming pool. Graham pointed her in the direction of the girls changing rooms, heading off himself in the opposite direction. Anna was feeling a bit intimidated but was determined not to show it and she pushed open the door of the changing rooms.

There were a couple of girls inside, drying off after their swim, and they both scrutinised Anna. 'We haven't seen you around before. Are you a new girl?' one of them said.

'No,' Anna said, imitating the girl's posh accent. 'I'm a guest of Graham Frost.'

'You know Graham?' the other girl said excitedly.

'Yes, I'm staying with him for a while actually.'

'You lucky devil! You know he's the captain of our swimming team, don't you?'

'No, I didn't know that. But he doesn't frighten me. I'm not a bad swimmer myself.'

Then, having changed quickly and carrying her towel, she left the two girls and pushed open the door to the pool itself. She almost said 'Wow!' again but reminded herself that she was *not* going to be intimidated. In front of her was what looked like an Olympic-sized pool, marked out in lanes, with a high diving board at one end. She was sure she had never swum in a pool like this. It was almost empty except for a couple of boys about Graham's age lazily doing lengths but swimming easily and strongly. Everything seemed to be new. There was no sign of dirt anywhere, unlike in the council pool where she usually swam, which was getting very shabby.

Graham was waiting for her at one end and she looked at his lean body in its swimming trunks as she approached, seeing that he had a good physique for a swimmer. She said, almost accusingly, 'You didn't tell me you were the captain of your school swimming team.'

'I didn't think it was relevant,' he said. 'Who've you been talking to?'

'Oh, a couple of girls in the changing rooms. They asked me if I was a new girl and I told them I was your guest.'

'Good thinking. I forgot to tell you to say exactly that if anybody questioned your presence. It would have been embarrassing if you'd been thrown off the premises as a gatecrasher before you'd even had a swim.' And he smiled his wicked grin again.

She grinned back and then said, 'OK. Let's swim, shall we?' And she dived cleanly into the water, starting a fast crawl down one of the empty lanes. She heard Graham dive in behind her and, to her amazement, just a few seconds later, he caught up with her and effortlessly overtook her. She maintained her own speed and reached the other end where Graham was waiting patiently for her.

'You *are* fast, aren't you?' she said admiringly.

'For a girl you're not bad yourself,' he replied and, knowing he was teasing her, she splashed water into his face. They frolicked around for a bit and then Anna said challengingly, 'Bet you can't keep that pace up over two lengths.'

Graham looked serious for a moment and then said, 'You're right. I probably can't. My distance is 40 metres. But I'm willing to give it a try.'

They hauled themselves out of the pool and sat on the

edge panting slightly. 'Come on then,' said Anna after a long pause and they both got into diving crouches. 'One, two, three, go!' and they dived in simultaneously. Graham took off like a rocket, his slim tall frame cleaving through the water like a porpoise while Anna was content to up her pace a little but not to overdo it. She knew distance was her strength and she was fairly sure Graham would tire before the two lengths were up. At the end of the first length, she saw he was less than a quarter of a length in front of her. He turned cleanly and, as he passed her, he grinned mischievously. Anna too made a good turn and now upped her pace. She could see Graham visibly slowing in front of her and that encouraged her. She caught up to him just before the end of the second length and her fingers touched the lip of the pool just before his. She whooped and, savouring her triumph, said, 'See?'

'Perhaps I let you win,' Graham said dejectedly but he was panting heavily. 'Wanna try it again?' Anna said, grinning at him but panting also. And Graham held up his hands in surrender, saying, 'No, thanks. I'm shattered.' And he looked at her with new respect.

They clambered out of the pool, sitting at the edge and dangling their toes in the water, and one of the two boys, who'd been in the pool originally and had been observing the race, clapped and called out, 'Who's your friend, Graham? Talk about the tortoise and the hare! We could do with her on the team.'

'I know, Jack. But I'm afraid we're not going to get her,' Graham called back.

Now Anna said, 'By the way, I'm on my school team too

but I'm not the captain yet. Maybe next year if I ever get to be more popular.'

'Why aren't you popular?' Graham asked.

'I think it's because I'm considered a swot and too much of a loner. For example, I never go to the school discos and I hate team sports.'

'Just like me,' Graham said in reply.

Then they went back to the changing rooms, agreeing that they'd both had enough hard exercise for one afternoon. While Anna was in the shower, she suddenly realised that she hadn't thought about her mother all afternoon and the thought made her feel guilty at first. So, when she came out, she checked her mobile but there were no messages. That meant there was no change so there was nothing to feel guilty about, was there? She was confused but determined not to lay her confusion on Graham or anybody else for that matter. She checked her appearance in the mirror before she left and was gratified to see that she looked OK. Her cheeks had a healthy flush from the exercise and even her zits appeared less prominent. Her hair glowed from the shampoo and, as it was still damp, it didn't look as frizzy as it normally did. But she never usually cared much about her appearance. So why did she care now? Was it just because of Graham? And then, being honest with herself, she realised it was.

She'd been alone in the changing rooms this time and when she came out, she met Graham in the corridor. 'Let's do that tour now, shall we?' he said and Anna agreed. So they went back to the main building and in through a side door.

Graham showed her what he called the refectory first. It was a huge room with many old paintings of serious-looking elderly gentlemen on the wood-panelled walls. There were long, dark, oak tables covering most of the floor area with benches alongside them and a kind of raised dais at one end with its own table and proper chairs, which was where the masters sat during meal times, Graham explained. Anna reckoned it looked very forbidding and gloomy, reminding her of the dining room at Hogwarts, Harry Potter's school, but without the colour and excitement, and about as unlike her own modern, light canteen as it was possible to get. But perhaps she was being too negative. After all, it was empty, wasn't it, and she presumed it would be different when it was full of noisy students.

After that he took her to the chapel which was adjacent to the school although it could also be reached from within it. It looked equally dead to Anna's eyes, being also wood-panelled with carved, choir stalls, the big altar at one end and its high dark wood ceiling. The only thing which relieved the gloom, in her opinion, was the gold-painted organ, which was raised up high at the opposite end from the altar. But she said nothing to Graham about these misgivings, assuming he was proud of his school and not wanting to offend him.

Then they went to the school hall with its large permanent stage for performances and raised tiers of seating but also panelled in dark wood with more paintings of old men on the walls. She realised then that the school was all about history and the past, although she suspected it was schools like this which bred the leaders of the future. It made her feel even more insecure to think that these leaders would probably come mainly from the wealthy classes, which she knew realistically she had no chance of joining.

After that she was taken up a magnificent flight of stairs to one of the dormitories where the boarders slept, except for those in the 6th form, he explained, who had their own rooms. Anna peered curiously behind a couple of curtains into the cubicles with their beds and lockers next to them and wondered to herself how any parent could send their child away to a place like this. To her it looked soul-destroying, like being in the army.

Then they went and looked out of a big window at one end of the long room and saw below them a cricket match in progress between two teams of young boys, all dressed in white. She knew nothing about the rules of the game but to her it appeared extremely boring although the boys seemed to be enjoying it. They watched for a while and then Graham asked, 'What else would you like to see?'

'Can I see your classroom?'

'Sure,' he said.

So they walked downstairs again and into another long, wide corridor until Graham came to a door. He opened it and they went in. Anna's first reaction was one of recognition as it looked pretty much like her own classroom. But then she saw that it was quite a bit smaller, in fact with only about twenty desks and chairs and roughly the same number of computers around the walls. There was the usual whiteboard at the front but the main difference she noticed was the view from the window. It looked over a stunningly beautiful garden, rather than an asphalt playground like hers did. She stared at this for a few moments and then decided that the view summarised nicely the deep gulf between the privileged few and the rest of the population. Could she *ever* be real friends with a posh boy like Graham, she wondered. However, she just asked him how many students there were in his class and he told her there were eighteen at present.

'There are thirty four in mine,' she said in a rather bitter tone.

But he seemed not to notice her bitterness and said, 'I'd like to show you our science labs last, OK?' Anna was not sure if she could take much more of the privilege on show here but meekly said, 'OK.' So Graham took her outside to one of the outbuildings, this one, however, bigger than the others. They went in and peered through a small window in the door at rank upon rank of expensive-looking equipment, much of which Anna didn't recognise. 'That's our chemistry lab,' Graham said with a note of pride in his voice. 'I'm afraid all the labs are locked outside lesson time. I suppose it's to stop the boys building a nuclear device in them.'

'Very nice,' Anna said shortly, not responding to his humour.

'What's the matter, Anna?' Graham said, this time recognising her tone.

'If you came to my school, you'd understand,' she replied shortly. 'Can we go now please? Your school's given me a lot to think about.'

'Of course,' he said and they went back without talking to where they'd left their bikes chained in a shed near the swimming pool. Anna had been thinking that she really shouldn't take out her feelings about the additional chances in life money provides on Graham and said brightly, 'Where is everybody?' They'd met no adults on their tour and had seen just a few of the younger boarders.

Graham seemed to be cheered by her new tone and answered, 'The masters are presumably all in their houses although there'll be some adults around, for example, in the kitchen but they're just the cooks and so on.' Anna caught the tone of snobbery in this remark and looked sharply at him but he ignored the look and continued, 'Most of the boarders will either be out playing sports or working in the library or perhaps in the city if they're old enough. It is Saturday, remember. Oh, I forgot to show you the library, didn't I?'

'Don't worry. Maybe next time,' she said, forcing a smile at him.

'I would like to go to your school, Anna,' he said and she realised that he was still worrying about her earlier sharp words.

'There's nothing much to see, I'm afraid.'

'Never mind. I'd still like to go.'

'Maybe I'll take you some day,' she said and he had to be content with that.

They cycled back to his house and, on their arrival, Graham said, 'Give me your wet things and I'll put them in the dryer.'

'OK. Thanks. I think I'll go up to my room for a bit,' Anna replied and left him in the hallway, holding her wet towel and swimming costume. When she got to her room, she checked her mobile again but there were still no messages. How long am I going to have to wait for Mum to wake up, she thought miserably. Then she thought to ring the hospital herself which she did. But they just said there'd been no change and she hung up feeling thoroughly depressed.

Chapter 8

Anna scrutinised herself in her bathroom mirror. The mirror in the changing room hadn't lied. Her zits were definitely less prominent now, looking like no more than a few rough bumps on her face. She wondered why all the expensive creams she'd plastered on it during the previous year and which, she reminded herself, her mother had paid for, hadn't worked but now, with no help at all, they'd almost vanished so quickly. It was a mystery. Surely it couldn't be the distress of what had happened?

She was interrupted in her musings by a knock on the door. It was Graham asking if she was hungry as he was going down to the kitchen to have some tea. 'Coming,' she said, suddenly realising that she was indeed hungry after all her exercise that afternoon. So they went together downstairs and found Gemma in the kitchen starting to make some pastry. She asked Anna how the afternoon had gone and Graham answered for her, saying, 'We had a race and she beat me.'

'Yes, but you're much faster than me over short distances,' Anna said, adding, 'We had a tour of his school and it was most interesting. How was your aerobics class?'

'Unfortunately I can't go often enough for it to make

much difference to this,' Gemma replied, patting her ample waistline with a flour-stained hand.

'I guess you must be awfully busy being a nurse,' Anna said but Gemma only grimaced in reply.

Then Graham piped up, 'We're hungry. What's there to eat, Mum?'

'Well, you can raid the biscuit tin if you like and you should know how to make tea by now, shouldn't you?' But she smiled at him as she said this, taking the sting out of the sarcasm.

Anna said, 'I'm not very fond of tea, to be honest. Do you have any juice?'

And Gemma replied, 'Yes, there's some in the fridge. I did the shopping this morning.'

So she went to the cavernous fridge and, pouring herself a big glass of cold orange juice, drank it slowly savouring the flavour. Graham made a mug of tea for himself and brought over a large tin of biscuits which they both chomped away on.

'Don't spoil your dinners, will you?' Gemma said and Graham rolled his eyes at Anna, saying, 'Mothers! That's one of her favourite sentences. Is your mum the same, Anna?'

Anna laughed although the mention of her mother brought the sadness back again and replied, 'Yes, exactly the same. It must be something to do with being a mother.'

Graham grinned at her and Anna thought again how she liked making him smile and she was determined not to let her own problems interfere with the happiness of this family. She changed the subject asking, 'Did you actually want to go to your school, Graham, or did your parents make you?'

'That's an interesting question. Honestly I don't exactly

remember although I'm quite sure that, if I'd been forced to go as a boarder, I would have kicked up a hell of a fuss.'

Gemma interrupted now, saying, 'We would *never* have sent you away to school, Graham, but the fact that St Paul's was so close made it a good choice for us.'

'I guess being a day boy at a boarding school means you get the best of both worlds,' Anna said.

'Yes, Peter and I think so although Graham himself often grumbles about it. At least you're getting a good education there, aren't you, Graham? Better than either of your parents got anyway. You must admit that.'

Why can't *I* have a good education too, Anna thought bitterly, thinking, unfairly she knew, that this was the first time Gemma had been less than a hundred per cent tactful.

'Yes, I suppose so,' Graham admitted grudgingly, adding, 'But I've really missed having any girls around me during my education.' And they left the topic there, turning the conversation to less controversial matters. Then Graham, who'd by now finished his tea, asked Anna if she'd like to come up to his room and she replied that she'd love to have a go with his train set.

It did not feel strange or threatening this time to be invited into a boy's room alone and, when they got there, he switched it all on and with a complicated remote control made the trains and wagons go flying around the tracks through stations and tunnels and over bridges. Anna watched fascinated, seeing the signals change from red to green as the trains went through them and watching how they slowed right down if there was oncoming traffic. Then Graham passed her the remote control, showing her how to use it, and she played around with the set for a while, fumblingly at first but soon getting the hang of the basics. She asked if he'd built it all on his own and he told her Peter had helped with the initial construction although he'd added a lot of refinements himself since then.

'This really is fun,' she said, adding wistfully, 'I wish I had something like this at home.'

'It took a lot of work,' Graham said, 'but I think it's come out rather well.'

Anna agreed heartily with that. Then she took her mobile out of her pocket and checked for messages again but there were still none. Graham said, 'I know this is a daft thing to say, Anna, but try not to worry too much about your mum. She's in the best of hands.'

She blinked tears out of her eyes and said coldly, 'I hope you haven't forgotten what you said at the hospital about tearing your hair out by now if it'd been your parents.' And, despite knowing that she was being unfair, she stalked angrily out of his room, thinking what a useless comment he'd made, and went back to her own, vowing to herself to go every day to the hospital to spend time with her mother. She knew she was ruining a possible friendship but also that she had to focus on her mother, not Graham, so it didn't really matter.

Then she remembered her school and how she had to phone them. So she dialled the number and a voice mail message gave her an emergency number to call as it was the weekend and she hesitantly dialled that instead. To her relief it was one of her favourite teachers, Mr Turner, who answered. She explained briefly what had happened and there was a shocked silence at the other end. He said, 'How awful,

Anna! Of course you must take as much time off school as you think you need. I'll tell all your teachers. Would you like us to e-mail you what we're doing in class and any homework?'

'Yes, please,' Anna said, glad of his understanding and sympathy. After a few more commiserations from Mr Turner, she hung up. Another thing taken care of, she thought.

Then she thought of her mother's friends and clients and wondered how she could contact them. She didn't have any of their numbers in her mobile. But she suddenly remembered that her mother had a Rolodex at home in which she kept all her important phone numbers and decided that tomorrow she'd go by the house and retrieve it.

She lay on her bed and thought this was indeed a crash course in growing up but knew it was one she wouldn't have wished on her worst enemy. She wondered what else she had to do but couldn't think of anything of immediate urgency. She knew she'd also have to bring all her school books back to the house tomorrow as she didn't want to get behind with her work. Then she just fell asleep, exhausted by the day and all she'd done.

She was woken by Gemma knocking on her door and calling her to supper so she went into her bathroom, washed her face and hurried back downstairs where she found the family just sitting down to eat. Graham eyed her cautiously, obviously wondering why his words of sympathy had made her leave his room so precipitously, but she didn't enlighten him and he didn't ask. She wanted no more conversation about her mum at present.

They ate well as usual and talked about trivial things, which suited Anna fine. At the end of the meal Graham asked her if she fancied playing snooker for a bit, clearly having decided to forgive her for her previous behaviour. She herself wanted to make it up to Graham now and admitted she'd never had the chance to play it although she'd watched it occasionally on the TV at the end of some important championship or other. 'Come along then. I'll teach you,' Graham said. She looked at Gemma, who said, 'Don't worry about the clearing up. It won't take long for Peter and me to do it.'

So she followed Graham out of the kitchen to the large games room, which seemed to have a floor area bigger than her whole house. As well as having a full-size snooker table in it, it also had a table tennis table and a huge plasma TV screen with lots of video games scattered around. She allowed Graham to show her the basic rules of snooker and they played for a bit after he'd shown her how to hold the cue. But, in spite of the fact that Graham was a patient teacher, she found the geometry needed to master the angles too complicated and eventually gave up.

'Let's play table tennis,' she said. It was an individual game she enjoyed and they were soon bashing the ball back at each other as hard as they could. Finally they both got tired and sat on the floor. 'What else are you good at?' Graham asked and Anna smiled at him and said, 'Not much. Can you show me the games?' waving her hand at the video games lying on the floor. So he showed her a few of them. Most of them she'd never heard of but once she'd had them explained to her, she thoroughly enjoyed playing them on the big TV screen. This was because they weren't the normal kind of Shoot-up-the-baddies games the boys at her school liked but actually required intelligence to solve the puzzles they presented.

Finally, she yawned and said, 'I'm off to bed, Graham,' and, once again, she thought she caught a look of disappointment in his eyes. She left him playing and went back to the kitchen, wanting to say goodnight to his parents, but neither of them were there. Then she heard the sound of a TV coming from down the hallway and went to investigate. She found his parents in the small cosy sitting room she'd peered into the day before with just space for a little sofa and an armchair and a smallish TV. She said her goodnights and they wished her sweet dreams.

After that, she traipsed upstairs to her room, undressed, put her pyjamas on, got washed and then lay down on her bed listening to the sounds of the big house settling down for the night. The moonlight shone through a gap in her curtains and she thought again of her mother. 'What are you dreaming about?' she asked her, trying to use telepathy to get through to her, but got no reply and finally dropped into a fitful sleep.

She woke up fully once in the middle of the night after another nightmare with her sheets and duvet all tangled around her, sweating profusely as if she had a high fever. She remembered every detail of it this time. She and her mother were on the deck of a ship during a storm and suddenly a huge wave came and knocked her mother overboard. She cried out but her mum was swept away by the force of the water. She shuddered at the memory and hoped it wasn't an omen. She got up, went into the bathroom and splashed cold water over her face. Then, having rearranged the bedding, she lay down again, trying to think only happy thoughts about the past and the future when her mum got better, and eventually managed to drop off.

CHAPTER 9

Anna woke up on Sunday morning, feeling slightly muzzy-headed and still distressed, and got dressed. Then she looked at her watch and was astonished to see it was still only 7 o'clock. So she lay down again and tried to doze but soon gave up and decided to check her e-mails on her laptop. She knew her school wouldn't have sent her any messages yet about school work but she thought that maybe somebody had heard about what had happened and would try to get in touch with her. But there were only a couple of spam e-mails which she deleted. After that she checked her mobile, which she had charged overnight, for messages but again there were none. She started to feel very isolated from the world and wished she had a close mate she could talk to about everything, something she'd never really missed before. But she pulled herself together and decided to try to read a book. However, she found she couldn't concentrate and quickly gave up.

Then she thought a walk around the big back garden she could see from her window but which she hadn't yet seen from ground level, might help her mood. So she slipped out of her room and went noiselessly downstairs. The family still seemed to be asleep as she could hear nothing from either Graham's or his parents' rooms. Going to the kitchen, she unlocked the back door with the key she found in the lock and went outside. It was perfectly silent there with not a cloud in the sky and she stood for a moment surveying the lawn, the flower beds and the huge, old trees. Then she set off walking across the lawn, which felt like velvet under her feet. In spite of the garden's size it didn't take her long to do a complete circuit, savouring the scents of the flowers and the herbs, which had their own patch of earth devoted to them, along the way. The short walk did indeed seem to have calmed her down and she felt more positive as she re-entered the kitchen.

Gemma was there, wearing her dressing gown, and she smiled at Anna saying, 'I saw you walking from our window. I find it very peaceful out there.' Anna agreed and asked if she could have a glass of juice. 'You don't have to ask, you know. This is as much your house now as it is ours,' Gemma said. Anna thanked her and poured herself a glass from the fridge. 'When I'm at home on Sunday, I usually prepare a proper breakfast for the family. Are you hungry, Anna?'

Anna considered the question. She decided that in fact, despite her continued distress, she was, in fact, quite hungry. So she replied, 'That'd be lovely, Gemma. Can I help?' Gemma declined her offer, saying it was an easy job, so Anna just sat there, drinking her juice and watching Gemma's, brisk, efficient movements. Then she asked, 'What does Graham usually do on Sundays?'

'Oh, he usually stays in his room all day doing his homework and playing with that computer he's trying to build.'

'OK. I'd like to go to the hospital by myself this morning on the bike. There's not much traffic around on Sundays and

I'm sure I'll be safe. On the way back I have to drop in at my house to pick up the rest of my school books. Oh, yes. I forgot to tell you. I phoned my school last night and spoke to one of my teachers. He was very understanding and said it was no problem my taking time off school and he promised he would e-mail me what my class are doing and any homework we're set.'

'That was very proactive of you, Anna. I'm impressed.'

Anna ignored the compliment and asked instead, 'By the way, do you, by any chance, have any panniers for the bike as the books are rather heavy and I won't be able to carry them all in my rucksack in one go?'

'Somewhere, yes. I think they're in the garage. I'll need to dig them out. I used them for the shopping in the good old days before I got too lazy to go on my bike and started driving everywhere.'

Anna smiled and said, 'Thanks again.'

They were silent for a while as Gemma prepared toast, fried eggs, bacon and coffee. Then she asked Anna to go and call the boys to the table. So she went back upstairs and knocked first on Peter and Gemma's bedroom door, delivering the message through the closed door. 'Coming,' she heard him say. Then she did the same at Graham's room and heard a grumbled, 'On my way.'

Back downstairs Gemma was already putting the food onto plates and Anna sat down, eyeing it hungrily. Peter and Graham soon turned up, also in their dressing gowns, and they all tucked in. Graham didn't say anything until he had finished his cup of coffee but then sat back, gave a discreet belch, which brought a disapproving look from his mother, and looked at Anna. 'What do you want to do today?' he asked.

'I was telling your Mum that I'd like to cycle to the hospital by myself this morning. Then I have to drop in at the house to pick up some stuff. I'll be back by lunchtime.'

'OK. What about this afternoon?'

'I haven't thought that far ahead. Any suggestions?'

'We could go for a cycle ride together. I know some nice parks not far away which sometimes have live music in them on Sundays.'

'Maybe. I'll see.' And they left it there.

After breakfast and helping Gemma clear up, Anna returned to her room, got her mobile, her house key and her rucksack and tidied up. Then she came down and went out of the back door to the shed where the bike was waiting for her. She wheeled it around to the front of the house and went back inside to the kitchen. There she found Gemma dressed and writing what she presumed was a shopping list and asked her if she could find the panniers for her. 'Are you ready to go?' Gemma asked. Anna nodded and Gemma got up and went outside with her to the garage where she rummaged around behind where she'd taken the bike from. Then she turned and exclaimed triumphantly, 'Here they are!' She carried them back to the bike and tied them on, making sure they were secure. 'Be careful. You've got the phone number of the house if you need to call us, don't you?' she said. 'Oh, no. I forgot to ask you for it,' Anna replied. So Gemma gave it to her and Anna keyed it into her mobile. 'Thanks again, Gemma,' she said and set off along the quiet Sunday streets to the hospital.

The journey was uneventful and she arrived after about twenty minutes. She chained the bike in a big lean-to near the main entrance where there were many other bikes already parked and went in. Her nose was immediately assailed by the odour of the big hospital, a mixture of cleaning products and sick people, and she thought again how warm it was inside. She knew the way to the ward by now and pressed the bell when she got there. She gave her name when asked and the door clicked open. Going straight down the corridor to her mother's room, she peered through the little window and was relieved to see her mum was alone. Getting a new mask and gown, she went in and looked at her mother who appeared to be sleeping peacefully with a slight smile on her face. She still had the huge bandage covering her head with the mask over her face and all the machines she was wired up to. Anna looked at the flat lines moving across one of the screens and noticed that there was a small blip which appeared regularly. She wondered if it was her breathing she was looking at as her chest was rising and falling almost in time with the blips.

She bent over her mother and, taking her mask off momentarily, kissed her on the cheek but there was no reaction. So she sat down next to her and, holding her hand, she started talking to her about what she'd done the previous day after she'd left her. She told her about Graham's school in as much detail as she could remember and about her confused emotions there. Then she talked about Graham himself and her mixed-up feelings for him, something she knew she'd never have done if her Mum hadn't been in a coma. Before, she'd prided herself on being able to talk to her mother about absolutely anything but now she knew she had a private area of her life which she'd have to keep to herself.

During all this she'd been observing her mum closely and she suddenly noticed her eyelids starting to flicker. She at once got very excited, wondering if perhaps she was waking up and who to ask about it. Then she remembered the red alarm button next to the bed. She pressed it once urgently and a nurse she knew appeared almost immediately.

'What's the problem, Anna?' the nurse asked.

She burst out, 'I saw my mum's eyelids flicker! Does that mean she's waking up?' But then she looked at her mother again and saw her eyes had settled back into the normal quiet expression of repose and didn't move again.

The nurse checked one of the monitors and gave Anna a pitying look and then an explanation of how it was a kind of involuntary, muscular spasm, which was perfectly normal in her mum's condition. Anna couldn't help feeling devastated but tried not to show it.

So then, to take her mind off her mother's plight, she asked about the functions of the machines crowded around her bed. She was told that, of the three most important, one was keeping an eye on the intravenous feeding tube leading into her body, another was monitoring her heart beat and the third, and probably the most important, was monitoring her brain activity. She asked if the machine doing the brain monitoring was the one with the blips on the screen and the nurse said, 'Yes, exactly. We'll make a nurse of you yet, Anna.'

Anna grimaced and said, 'No, thanks.' But then she asked, 'And the mask presumably is for oxygen?'

'Yes,' the nurse replied simply. All this while she was busy taking her mother's temperature and blood pressure and checking the wires leading into her body and the screens for anomalies. She added a number of short notes to her mother's medical chart and then turned to Anna and said, 'I'm sorry but I have to go now. I have more patients to see but I'll come back later if you want.'

'That's OK,' Anna said. 'I'll be leaving fairly soon myself. Thanks for the information.' The nurse smiled at her and left.

She continued sitting there holding her mother's hand, talking to her about whatever came into her head. But finally the words dried up and she felt like crying again. She sat for a bit longer and then looked at her watch. She was surprised to see that it was already 11.30. She reluctantly let go of her mother's hand and stood up. 'I have to go now, Mum,' she said. 'I promised Mrs Frost that I'd be back by lunchtime and I still have to go by the house to pick up my school books. I'd also like to check your Rolodex for Serena's and Miriam's phone numbers so that I can tell them what's happened as well as those of your latest clients if I can find them. I'll come and see you again tomorrow. OK?' But again there was no reaction and she picked up her rucksack and with a last, sad, backwards look she left her mother's room.

She collected her bike from where she'd left it and cycled off to her own house through the still, almost-deserted streets. When she got there, she went in and noticed at once how musty it was already getting inside so she went around opening as many windows as she dared without letting burglars in. Then she collected all her relevant school books from her bedroom and put them on her bed. Next she went into her mother's bedroom and got the Rolodex from where it always sat on her mum's bedside table next to a telephone. She kept it well organised in different sections and she found Miriam's and Serena's numbers without difficulty.

She rang Miriam first on the land line and was relieved to find her in. She told her the news and there was a gasp of horror from the other end followed by a lot of questions which she answered as best she could. She told her about staying with Mrs Frost and assured her she was fine. Then, when she was asked, she gave her mum's ward number and the visiting hours to Miriam and she promised that she'd visit her very soon. Then she hung up and dialled Serena's number. She too was in and the conversation went almost identically to how it had with Miriam. When she finally managed to hang up, she was pleased she'd done that as she knew that Miriam and Serena moved in different circles but that together they'd quickly get the news out to her mum's other friends.

Then she moved on to the trickier task and looked in the Rolodex for her latest clients. She quickly found two she thought sounded promising as she remembered her mum mentioning them both recently in relation to her work.

She rang the first and was answered by a shrill voice saying, 'Yes. Who is this?'

She gave her name and asked if her mother was still working for her.

'Indeed she is. Is there a problem?' the voice replied.

'Yes, I'm afraid so,' Anna said and repeated the news all over again.

There was a wail at the other end and the voice said in a

tone of pure exasperation, 'But what's going to happen to my house? She's still got the two most important rooms to do!'

What a bitch! Anna thought to herself but replied calmly, 'I have no idea but I thought you ought to know.'

The woman must have realised what she'd said because at least she apologised and finished by saying, 'Please ask Pauline to ring me as soon as she's able to,' and Anna promised she would.

She hung up, relieved that she'd survived the call, and then reluctantly rang the second name but this time there was no reply and no answer phone. So she copied the number onto a piece of paper along with the woman's name and slipped it into the front pocket of her rucksack. I've done as much as I can for now, she thought.

After all that she went back to her own bedroom and filled the rucksack with some of her books, carrying the rest outside and putting them in the panniers. Now heavily laden, she was ready to leave when their next-door neighbour, a Mrs Carrington, came out, carrying a watering can.

She called out to Anna, who turned from unlocking her bike, and said, 'Where's your Mum? I haven't seen her around for a few days.' So Anna had to run through the whole story yet again. 'I'm so very sorry. If there's anything at all I can do, please don't hesitate to ask,' her neighbour said when she'd finished speaking.

'Could you keep an eye on the house please? I'm not sure how long I'll be away,' Anna replied.

'Of course,' Mrs Carrington said. 'But how do I contact you if there is a problem?'

Anna dug her mobile out of her rucksack, tore off a strip

of paper from her exercise book and wrote down the number of Gemma's house, glad she had it. She handed this to Mrs Carrington, said her thanks and cycled away, feeling totally empty after all the social niceties she'd had to undergo. It was already nearly one o'clock, she noticed. She had to hurry. So she pedalled as fast as she could back to Graham's house, parking the bike outside the back door.

Chapter 10

Anna heard noises from the kitchen and went in, finding the family there, poised to eat. She was panting, feeling the sweat from the warm sunshine and the exercise trickling down her back and making her T-shirt stick to it. 'Hi, Anna,' Gemma called out as she entered, 'How did it go? You look hot. Sit down and I'll bring you a drink.'

'Did I miss lunch?'

'No, not at all. We're just about to eat.'

'I thought I was going to be late,' Anna said.

'Well, you're not.' And Gemma handed her a big glass of juice which she gulped down quickly. 'We usually eat late on Sundays if I'm around.'

'That just hit the spot,' Anna said gratefully, putting the empty glass down on the table.

'Good,' Gemma said, handing out plates laden with roast chicken, roast potatoes and vegetables. 'Here's the gravy.'

Anna looked at her plate hungrily but, before she started, she told the family a little about her morning, how her mother's condition hadn't changed and how she had made the important phone calls she had wanted to make from home.

'How did the cycling go?' Graham asked with his mouth full.

'Fine. No problems. The streets were very quiet.'

Then she started tucking in, enjoying every mouthful. There were big bowls of strawberries and ice cream for dessert and Anna ate everything, realising that the cycling had given her an appetite. The talking was desultory during lunch as the family were all concentrated on eating. But then, when everybody had finished, Peter sat back and said, 'Before you arrived, we were talking about what we could do as a family this afternoon. It's such a nice day it seems a pity to waste it here at home. Graham's done some Googling and told us that there's a free live jazz concert on in one of the parks not far away. I'd like to go. Would you like to join us?'

'I'd love to,' Anna replied. 'Have I got time for a shower first? I feel very sticky.'

'By all means,' Peter said looking at his watch, 'if you're not too long.'

'I won't be,' she promised. And she got up from the table, looking enquiringly at Gemma.

'Don't worry about things here. The boys will help me. You run along and get cleaned up. It doesn't matter if we arrive a bit late,' Gemma said.

'Thanks,' Anna said and left the kitchen. She went upstairs to her room and shut the door. She sat on the bed for a short while, thinking about her morning and, once again, about how quickly her life had changed. Then she got up and had a quick shower, washing her hair. She came out feeling clean and changed her clothes but, as she was in a hurry, forgot all about putting her mobile into her jeans pocket, leaving it on her bedside table. She combed her hair and finally looked in the mirror. She still looked pale but not too bad considering, she thought. Surely I should be looking haggard and wasted? But she didn't spend time worrying about it, instead going back downstairs. She met Gemma in the hallway.

'You look nice,' Gemma remarked and Anna thanked her. 'I'm just waiting for the boys. It takes them forever to get out of the house, especially when we're all going somewhere together.' Anna smiled, thinking how incongruous it was to call big, burly, bearded Peter a boy.

However, they both appeared not long after and they all piled into Gemma's small car and set off with Peter in the front passenger seat and she and Graham wedged together in the back. She could feel the heat of his thighs coming through her jeans but made no move to pull away. To distract herself, she asked Peter if he drove and he answered, 'I haven't driven for years. I don't really need to working from home. Gemma doesn't allow me to drive her car; I think she doesn't trust me.' In reply Gemma gave him a playful cuff round the ear and Peter let out a pretend yelp of pain saying, 'You see how she abuses me, kids. I should complain to the NSPCF, the National Society for the Prevention of Cruelty to Fathers.' That earned him another cuff and he said nothing else about the way his wife treated him.

Then Anna remembered what Graham had told her about Peter being in a jazz band long ago and she asked him about it. 'Yes, it's true,' he said, 'but it was so many millennia ago, way back in my dissolute youth and long before I met Gemma, that I don't remember much about it.'

'Come on, Peter! You're not that ancient!' Graham said crossly. 'Sure, the drugs and alcohol have probably addled your memories a bit but you're always regaling me with stories of those good old days in the band.'

'Yes, OK,' Peter admitted. And he went on to tell Anna how much fun it'd been touring around Britain with a bunch of his old university mates in the antique van they had and about the disasters on the road and at the places they played. He was very entertaining and Anna felt she could've gone on listening to him for ever.

'We're there, guys,' Gemma called out as she pulled over, parking behind a long line of cars lining the street opposite a park. They all got out and Anna could hear the music already, the bass thumping through the soles of her feet. 'Do you like jazz?' Peter asked her as they strolled together through the open gates.

'I don't know much about it,' Anna admitted hesitantly.

'Well, the group you're going to hear will be a reasonable introduction to it then, I think. They play mostly traditional stuff but in their own style, most of it from New Orleans and Chicago. Nothing too modern.'

Anna didn't reply, not wanting to expose her ignorance any further, and they went into the park until they came to a large area of open grass with a big crowd of people sitting around. The music was loud here, coming from big speakers set up on a stage about forty yards in front of them. They found themselves some open space and sat on the dry grass. Anna looked around. The crowd seemed to be predominantly older people in their 50's or 60's but with a large sprinkling of young couples too and even a few families with young children running around. All the adults appeared to be concentrating on the music and, when a tune ended, there was a big roar of appreciation from the crowd. Anna liked the almost sedate atmosphere. It felt safer than at the two or three rock concerts she'd been to in her life. She remembered going, at her insistence, to one the previous year with her mother in a big hall and she would never forget the band members, heedless of their safety, crowd surfing off the stage into the audience.

She lay back on the grass and concentrated on the music, letting it wash over her and seep into her body and mind and she almost managed to forget everything that'd happened to her in the past couple of days. She could make out the melody quite clearly, even though it was embellished with a lot of improvisation, and she noticed Peter and Graham drumming along on the grass with their fingers to the rhythm which seemed complicated to her, certainly more complicated than the rhythms of the pop music she'd always listened to in the past. The group itself comprised a pianist, a saxophonist, a bass guitarist and a drummer but no singer and she was amazed by the technical virtuosity they showed when they did their solos. But they played together well too and she realised that here was a whole new world of music waiting for her to explore.

For the next hour and a bit they lay there in the sunshine and listened and applauded, listened and applauded. For their finale the group did something called, according to Peter, 'Chicago Stomp' which got everybody up and dancing. Then after one final, short encore, the group packed away their instruments and left the stage. The four of them got up and followed Gemma out of the park.

'So what did you think?' Graham asked her.

'I think I'd like to know a lot more about jazz,' she told him boldly.

'I think that can be arranged,' he said, smiling at her. 'I'm glad you enjoyed it.'

'I enjoyed it much more than I thought I would, to be honest,' she said. 'It was fascinating as well as enjoyable.'

'We'll make a fan of you yet,' Graham said, smiling again. She grimaced, remembering the words of the nurse earlier, but then smiled back at him and they wandered back to the car, walking behind his parents and chatting about the concert and their impressions.

When they got home, Gemma said, 'Tea, anyone?' and the two 'boys' put their hands up in unison. So they all went to the kitchen where Gemma made tea for her family while she gave Anna another glass of juice. They dug into the big biscuit tin which was soon empty and, seeing the worried look on Graham's face as he ate the last one, Gemma said, 'Don't worry. There are plenty more in the larder.'

Graham looked relieved and turned to Anna. 'I've still got to finish off my homework. How about you?'

'There are still a few things I need to do myself,' she replied.

'OK. How about we meet up later then,'

'Sure,' Anna said as she got up from the table. Then she remembered that she still hadn't emptied the books from the panniers on her bike or put it away. 'Can you help me carry my school books upstairs?' she asked Graham. 'No problemo,' he said and they went through the back door to where she'd left the bike. They took all the books out of the panniers and put them on the kitchen table while Anna went back outside and put the bike away in the shed, locking it carefully.

She was relieved it hadn't been stolen while they'd been at the concert but then she supposed that there wasn't much crime in this neighbourhood. It wasn't like her own street where you couldn't leave anything outside for long without it disappearing, even the milk from the doorsteps. But she still resolved never to forget to lock the bike again.

When she went back in, she was surprised to see that the big pile of books was no longer on the kitchen table but Gemma said, 'Graham's just taken the last lot upstairs. I'm glad the panniers came in useful.'

'I couldn't have done it without them,' Anna said, smiling at her.

But, despite her better mood, there was real danger for her mother lurking just around the corner.

CHAPTER 11

Anna returned to her room where she found all the books piled on her bed but no sign of Graham. Then she noticed her mobile phone, which she'd left lying on the bedside table. 'How could I possibly have forgotten that?' she thought angrily and she knew inside that, although she'd been in a hurry, that wasn't really an excuse. It was because of the prospect of an afternoon with Graham listening to music and she immediately felt guilty for letting her mother down so quickly. She went straight over to it and checked it for messages and was surprised to see that there was one, sent just about half an hour before. She opened it at once and saw that the hospital had been trying to call her. 'Oh, God, no!' she said out loud.

When she dialled the number, she got somebody who said with some urgency, 'Could you possibly come in as your mother has a few problems and we'd like you to be there just in case?'

In case of what? Death? Anna thought, panic-stricken. 'Can you give me any details?' she asked, her voice trembling.

'No, I'm sorry; I'm just passing on a message from the ward sister.'

'I'll be there as soon as I can!' Anna said in a frenzy and hung up.

She raced downstairs to the kitchen and told Gemma, sobbing, how she'd forgotten her mobile and what the hospital had said.

Understanding her distress, Gemma said decisively, 'I'll take you there now.'

'*Thank* you, Gemma,' Anna said with feeling.

Together they ran out to the car, Gemma stopping just long enough to tell Peter what'd happened. They raced over to the hospital, breaking the speed limit all the way but weren't stopped. When they arrived, Anna didn't even wait for Gemma to lock the car but bounded out and ran straight for the front door. She raced upstairs, not bothering with the lift as it seemed to be taking ages to come and there were many people waiting. She was feeling guiltier by the second that she had been out enjoying herself when her mum needed her.

Arriving at the ward, she pressed the bell frantically and was admitted, as usual, after giving her name. She flew down the corridor and came to her mother's room, panting heavily. Barging in, she saw her mum surrounded by two nurses and a doctor. The nurses were anxiously watching the heart monitor while the doctor was fiddling with something that looked like the oxygen supply. They looked up surprised at her entrance but then one of the nurses she recognised form the day before said, 'Oh, hello. You're the daughter, aren't you?'

'Yes,' replied Anna shortly. 'Can somebody *please* tell me what's going on?'

The doctor replied, 'We're not exactly sure but your mum's heart beat suddenly became very erratic and we were afraid she might be having a heart attack. So we've increased her oxygen and added a drug to stabilise it.'

A heart attack? On top of everything else? Anna didn't know how much more she could stand and sat down heavily on one of the chairs. She just couldn't take it in.

Then the doctor added, 'It seems to be working.'

Only seems? Anna thought she might start howling at any moment. But then Gemma appeared and took charge. She questioned the nurses and doctor closely about exactly what had happened. They seemed to be in some awe of her, even the doctor, and answered all her questions carefully. Anna, however, had tuned everything out and was sitting listlessly in the chair, looking at her mother, who seemed to be having some trouble breathing. She knew she should make the effort to put on a mask and gown but she didn't have the energy and nobody was forcing her.

Finally Gemma turned to Anna and said, speaking slowly, 'Well, Anna, all the procedures have been followed and the prognosis is now much better than it was. Unfortunately, medicine is not an exact science. That's why sometimes we just have to guess what the best treatment should be. It makes it more difficult that we can't ask your mum how she's feeling. But she seems to be recovering well now.'

Only 'seems' again! There were simply too many uncertainties! But Anna knew she had to leave matters in the hands of the professionals. So she just said, 'Is there anything I can do?'

'No, not really,' Gemma replied. 'We just have to wait and hope there's no recurrence of the problem. I think it's best if you come home with me and leave the doctors and nurses to do their jobs. They'll let you know how things are going.'

'OK,' Anna said reluctantly. She didn't want to leave her mum alone again but knew that Gemma was right. So she hoisted herself out of the chair and, with a squeeze of her mother's hand, followed Gemma back out of the ward.

When they got back to the car, Gemma inspected her closely and then said, 'I do hope you're not going to blame yourself too much for forgetting your mobile this afternoon. It was my fault as much as yours. I should have reminded you to bring it.'

'But I still shouldn't have forgotten it!' Anna wailed.

'Maybe not. But you couldn't have done much anyway, could you?'

'I guess not,' Anna said, grateful to Gemma for her sensibleness. 'I think I need to learn to pray properly,' a statement which surprised her as soon as she'd said it.

'Try not to worry too much, Anna. The hospital won't let anything really bad happen to your mum.' And on that note she drove home.

When they got back, Anna went straight up to her room and lay sobbing on her bed. Then, when she'd run out of tears and feeling totally emotionally shattered, she closed her eyes, drifting off quite quickly into sleep in spite of the strong sunlight still showing through her big window as she hadn't bothered to close the curtains.

When she finally woke up, it was dark outside and Anna had lost all track of time. She looked at her watch and saw it was 9 o'clock already. So presumably she'd missed dinner. She really didn't care about this as she seemed to have completely lost her appetite and was grateful to Gemma for not waking her earlier. Again she thought about forgetting her phone and realised she was thoroughly, if unfairly, resentful of Graham for distracting her from what must be her primary concern, her mother, and she promised herself faithfully it wouldn't happen again. She thought she'd have to steer clear of Graham for the time being and that thought made her strangely sad.

Then she tried to remember what she still had to do and suddenly it came back to her. She was going to ring that other client of her mum's. So she took the number out of her rucksack and dialled it. This time a lady replied in an aristocratic voice saying, 'Yes, can I help you?' Anna went through the whole routine again of introducing herself and telling her what'd happened. But this time the lady was very sympathetic and just said when Anna had explained, 'I'm so sorry. Well, it can't be helped. Thank you very much for letting me know,' and rang off. Anna put the phone down, relieved that it hadn't been another bitch like the first client. She thought how much easier it'd be if her mum wasn't freelance, if she could just ring an office, tell somebody once about it and be done with it. But then she thought that, as far as she knew, her mother had only had the two clients at the moment. However, she still reminded herself to check the answer phone at the house every so often for messages.

But what if her mum actually died? She'd considered the possibility before but now it seemed much nearer, not nearly so abstract. She decided to ring the ward to find out if there was any more news. When she did so, she was thankful it was the same nurse who'd been treating her mother earlier who answered. She told Anna that everything now appeared stable but they were keeping a close eye on her.

'You will ring me at once if there's any change, won't you?' Anna asked pleadingly and the nurse promised that she would and hung up.

There was nothing else she could do now except pray and she didn't feel like doing that. She was too angry with God for putting her through all this. So she went into her bathroom and washed her face, not even bothering this time to look in the mirror. She didn't want to see what she looked like. Then she thought that she should tell Gemma what the hospital had said so she went downstairs to look for her.

She found her alone in the kitchen, clearing away the remains of the dinner, and Gemma at once said, 'I didn't want to wake you. Sleep is often the best medicine. Would you like something to eat now? A sandwich maybe?'

'No, thanks,' Anna replied. 'I'm not hungry. I just rang the hospital and came down to tell you what they said.'

After she'd delivered the nurse's short message, Gemma said, 'Well, that's encouraging.'

'I suppose so,' Anna answered miserably.

'Come here, child.'

And, when Anna went up to her, Gemma put her arms around her and gave her a big hug. Anna felt like crying again but fought back the tears and said with a sob in her voice, 'Thanks for that,' realising the hug was exactly what she'd needed and that it had indeed made her feel better. She said as much to Gemma and hugged her back.

'I always think there's not enough physical contact in the world today,' Gemma said.

'Will you be my mother if my real mum dies?' Anna asked plaintively, feeling the tears welling up again.

'Hush, Anna. Don't talk like that. Your mum's not going to die. But this is your second home now, remember. You can stay as long as you like.'

'Again, thank you, Gemma,' Anna said, hugging her tighter.

Finally they broke away from each other and Gemma said, 'Perhaps you should go back to bed. As I said, sleep is probably the best medicine for you now.'

'Yes, I'll do that. Thanks again, especially for the hug,'

Gemma smiled broadly at her and said, 'Any time,' and Anna managed a weak smile back.

She left the kitchen and wandered slowly back up to her bedroom, not bothering to say good night to Graham. There she got undressed and climbed into bed, still emotionally exhausted. She lay awake for ages thinking about her mother and the good times they'd had together and, finally, with those happy memories in her head, managed to doze off. She slept fitfully, however, waking up several times in the night thinking of her poor mother.

Chapter 12

When Anna woke up, she made a resolution. From today she would get into a routine and visit her mum in the morning and work on her school stuff all afternoon. If she did that, she reckoned she could easily keep up. She hoped that way she'd be able to take her mind off her mother, at least for short periods. She was still desperately worried about her and anxious to get over to the hospital. Then she remembered it was Monday which meant Graham should be at school all week. That should make it much easier to avoid him. She was determined not to be distracted by him at the moment although she knew she'd still have to be polite to him.

So after getting dressed, she went down to the kitchen but found it empty. She thought a stroll round the garden might help her mood, as it had before, so she went outside. However, there was a cold breeze and she came back in quickly and poured herself a glass of milk. Then Peter wandered in, carrying the morning paper, and said 'How are you feeling, Anna?' to which she just shrugged. He didn't attempt any more conversation but started making his morning coffee. He was followed closely by Graham, dressed very smartly in his school uniform. He made his own breakfast in silence and ate it quickly. She felt him looking at her but she didn't have the energy to make conversation with him.

Just before he left, he said to Anna, 'I'm off to school now. Are you sure you'll be OK?'

She was touched by his solicitousness and said, 'Yes, thanks. Where's your mum, by the way?'

Peter looked up from his bowl of cereal and said, 'She left ages ago for the hospital.'

'Oh,' Anna said, having forgotten or never having known that nurses worked strange shift patterns.

'I should be here all day,' Peter continued. 'What are your plans?'

'To go to the hospital myself. I should be back by lunchtime and I'll be here all afternoon doing my school work.'

'OK. We can have lunch together then.'

'That'll be nice,' Anna said politely.

Graham picked up his school bag and went out through the back door. She heard him unlocking his bike and wheeling it around to the front before cycling away.

Then Peter asked, 'How do you propose to get to the hospital?'

'I'd like to try going on the bike. It's by far the most efficient way to get there, much better than the bus, and I think I'm confident enough now.'

'OK. But be careful. Some of these city drivers are maniacs and sometimes don't even seem to see bicycles in their way.'

'I will. Don't worry.'

'While I'm in loco parentis, I'll always worry about you,' he said smiling. She managed a small smile back. By now he'd finished putting his dirty crockery and cutlery in the dishwasher and he turned and said, 'Well, I'm off to work. Not literally, fortunately. Help yourself to whatever you want.' 'Thanks,' she said and he too left. She made herself a big slice of toast and marmalade and washed it down with more milk, then went back upstairs and finished getting ready for the morning's expedition.

She threw on a jersey, unplugged her mobile from the charger where it had lain silent all night and took a note from the envelope Gemma had given her, figuring it was possible she might need some money today. Then she tidied her room and checked she had everything she needed in her rucksack, including her plastic raincoat, and went downstairs and through the back door. Getting the bike, she set off down the street which was much busier than it'd been the day before. Fortunately, it still wasn't raining and the tarmac was dry. She was a bit scared of the traffic and kept all her senses alert for danger but the journey passed uneventfully. She did, however, feel relieved when she got to the gates of the hospital, and she parked the bike where she'd put it the previous day.

She went through the big revolving doors at the main entrance of the hospital and made her way directly to her mother's ward. She was buzzed in and, as she walked down the corridor, she passed Gemma, wearing a dark blue uniform, talking to some younger nurses all in light blue. But she had her back turned to her and she didn't disturb her, walking instead straight down to her mother's room. There she peered through the window and saw a nurse plumping up the pillows behind her mother's head. She slipped on a mask and gown, knocked and went in. 'Can I help you?' the nurse said. She clearly didn't know who Anna was.

'That's my mother,' Anna replied.

'Oh,' the nurse said, obviously flustered. 'Come in and make yourself at home. I'm just leaving.'

'Thank you,' Anna said, putting her rucksack on the floor and pulling a chair up closer to the bed. 'Is there any improvement?'

'She seems to be over her problems of yesterday but you really need to ask Mr Penny when he does his ward round,' the nurse replied hesitantly.

'OK,' she said, peering into what she could see of her Mum's face and gripping her hand. Then she looked hard at the machines which were all beeping away as usual. The brain monitoring one still showed the same regular blips on the screen and this, in a strange way, somehow reassured her. It showed she wasn't any better but also no worse, at least as far as her brain went. Her heart, however, could be another matter.

The nurse left and Anna started talking. First she told her mum what an awful fright she'd given her yesterday and described what'd happened, not forgetting to mention her mistake with her mobile phone. Then she went on to say a short prayer for her mother's full recovery from her supposed heart attack, adding she hoped nothing like it would ever happen again. She found that in the hospital it was actually possible to pray, which, when she thought about it, she presumed was logical. After all, a hospital was where most people went either to die or to recover from something serious and, if you couldn't pray there, where could you?

Then she went on to tell her all about the concert of yesterday, her enjoyment of the music and her new interest in jazz. After that she continued by describing her increasingly complicated relationship with Graham and how she blamed him partly for making her forget her phone. She discovered that talking through all these things, even with her comatose mother who couldn't respond, helped her see them in a clearer light and rationalise them. This pleased her, especially when she realised that, in fact, Graham certainly wasn't to blame for her mother's condition and that she could safely renew her relationship with him.

Again when she finally ran out of things to say, she just recited the mantra in a whisper, 'You're going to get better! You're going to get better!' And again at one point her mother's eyelids flickered but, when she looked at the machine, all it showed was the same flat line, punctuated by the same occasional blips.

Then Mr Penny came in, accompanied by the usual gaggle of young doctors, and asked her to wait outside as he had done before. When he came out, he said in his usual clipped sentences, 'First, Miss Sixsmith, sorry about the shock you must've had yesterday. Fortunately, however, your mother appears to have made a full recovery from the heart problems. The tests we've run have all come back normal. The doctor on duty was very quick to react and gave her exactly the right drug to help her. Such things can sometimes happen as a direct result of the trauma of the surgery. Second, as you can probably tell, there's no improvement yet in her underlying condition but I wouldn't have expected one at this stage. I think her brain is probably resting while it rewires itself.

You're doing the right thing though, talking to her. Keep it up.' And with those words he strode off.

'Rewiring itself?' Anna thought wonderingly. 'Can a brain really do that?' and she resolved to do some research into the brain when she got home. She stayed a bit longer but, then, explaining to her mother what her plans were for the afternoon, she left her room and wandered disconsolately down the corridor. There she met Gemma who was just coming out of one of the big bays. She saw Anna, smiled and went up to her saying, 'I heard you were here. I was just about to pop in to check on your mother and you. I'm really glad, by the way, that your mum's got over her heart problems.'

'So am I' Anna said, brightening up at the sight of her. 'I've spoken to Mr Penny and was just leaving actually.'

Gemma looked at the watch pinned to her jacket and said, 'My. Is that the time already? Well, I've got to get on, Anna.'

'Before you go, I've just got a quick question for you, Gemma.' Anna said.

'Ask,' Gemma said, to Anna's ears in a rather Mr Penny-like way.

'Why do you wear a dark blue uniform while all the other nurses wear light blue ones?'

Gemma laughed. 'Oh, that's easy. I'm a ward sister when I'm here which means that I'm in charge of all these young things you've seen scurrying around.'

'Oh, really?' Anna said impressed, not having realised that there would be a hierarchy among nurses like everywhere else in society.

'Yes,' Gemma said, adding, 'I'll be home around 7 this evening. OK?'

'OK. See you then,' Anna called out at her retreating back.

She left the hospital and discovered it was drizzling a bit outside. 'Bloody English weather!' she thought, putting on her raincoat. She found the bike and cycled steadily and carefully home. It was interesting, she thought as she went in, dripping water all over the floor, that she already considered this house home.

She found Peter in the kitchen cutting bread for sandwiches with some soup bubbling away on the stove. He was wearing an apron and Anna almost felt like laughing but managed not to. She didn't want to offend him. 'Oh, good. There you are. It's not very nice out there, is it? How did it go at the hospital?' he said, busying himself with crockery and cutlery. And Anna told him the good news about the heart issue and what Mr Penny had said. 'I'm pleased about that. I guess you'll just have to be patient, though, until your mum wakes up,' he commented.

'I know I will,' Anna replied.

Then he put a bowl of soup in front of her and they started eating. When they had finished the soup, Anna asked Peter about something she'd been thinking about on the way home. 'How does Gemma cope with her emotions when a patient dies? It must be awful. I don't think I could do it.'

'Neither could I,' Peter said. 'Nursing's not for everyone. I asked Gemma the same question a long time ago and she told me it was something nurses and doctors simply had to learn how to do, how to divorce their emotions from the job without losing their humanity in the process. She said it was often a difficult balancing act but, until a nurse knew how to do it well, she couldn't call herself a proper nurse. What prompted the question?'

'I'm not sure. I guess it was simply seeing all those desperately sick people in the hospital.'

'It's not a nice environment for a young, healthy girl to have to visit every day,' Peter said sympathetically and Anna smiled gratefully at him.

They continued eating, Peter having laid a selection of things out for them to put in their sandwiches and they finished with a large, juicy apple each. 'That was yummy. Thanks,' Anna said as she collected the dirty things and put them in the dishwasher. Peter said nothing and left the kitchen, Anna presumed, to go back to work in his study.

When she'd tidied up, Anna took her rucksack and wet raincoat up to her room and then opened up her laptop which was on the desk. First she checked her e-mails and found she had lots, all from her teachers and classmates expressing their sympathy and commiseration. She thought that the ones from her classmates sounded a bit like 'There but for the Grace of God go I,' but she was pleased to get them anyway. However, she didn't respond to any of them.

Instead she Googled the human brain. All the technical stuff, however, was way beyond her until she hit upon a child's website where at last she found a much-simplified account of its workings. She read it through carefully and quickly discovered that the brain could indeed rewire itself after injury. She also discovered, to her dismay, that the left side was responsible for control over the right side of the body and was the more creative and imaginative half while the right controlled the other side of the body and was more academic and logical. She remembered it was the left side of her mum's brain which had been injured but, unfortunately, her mother's job relied almost solely on her creativity. What if she couldn't do it any longer after she recovered physically? She knew how devastated that would make her feel.

But then she thought again about the rewiring Mr Penny had mentioned and she felt somewhat reassured. But only somewhat for she also remembered what he'd said about how little doctors actually knew about the brain. Then, however, she decided that, as there was nothing she or anybody else could do, apart from what they were already doing, it was all in the lap of the Gods anyway. She'd just have to be patient, as Peter had said, and wait to see how it turned out.

She knew she had to turn now to her school work and she found, embedded in a couple of her Monday morning teachers' e-mails, instructions on what she should read and also a small amount of homework based on the reading. So she forced herself to concentrate and for the next hour or so worked on it until she was satisfied. Then she remembered a history essay she'd intended to do over the weekend and lost herself in that for a while. She reread it, made sure it was long enough and that she'd answered the question and e-mailed it off to her history teacher. It wasn't up to her usual high standards but she knew it would do.

She looked at her watch and saw it was 4.30. Enough work for one day, she thought and stood up and stretched. She wondered if Graham was back yet and went downstairs to see if she could find him. But there was no sign of him so she got herself a glass of juice and sat at the kitchen table, sipping it reflectively by herself. She noticed that the day was starting to clear up a bit outside and thought that he shouldn't be as wet as she'd been when she came home at lunchtime. He finally turned up at about 5 and explained that he'd had swimming practice after school as he usually did. He got himself a mug of tea and the tin of biscuits and, sitting opposite her, eyed her and asked, 'How did it go at the hospital?'

'OK, I guess,' she said but she didn't want to talk about it. Instead she asked, 'What did you study today?' And he told her his Monday timetable. Then she asked him lots more questions about his school work but it seemed that the year before he had covered almost exactly what Anna was doing at present, albeit at a slightly higher level, although now of course he was a year ahead of her and coming up to his GCSE's. They talked about these for a while, Anna explaining why she'd chosen the ones she had and Graham doing the same. Finally Graham stood up and said, 'I want to get out of these awful clothes and I need to have a think about some Maths homework.'

'Do you think you might be able to help me if I have a problem with my Maths? It's the most difficult subject for me,' Anna asked diffidently.

'I don't see why not,' he said, smiling at her.

She followed him slowly upstairs, went back to her room and got out a book. This time she had no trouble concentrating on it and soon lost herself in the plot. Later she heard Gemma come back and call out for Peter. So, remembering to put her mobile in her pocket, she went back downstairs and found her busy preparing supper. She helped her with it and they talked about this and that. Then Anna called the 'boys' down and they all sat down and ate. After they'd finished and cleared up and Peter had gone back to his work, Graham looked at Anna and said, 'Do you have anything important to do now?'

'No, I don't think so. Why?'

'Shall we go upstairs and I'll show you my CD collection?'

Anna thought this was the corniest pick-up line she'd ever heard but, when she looked at him closely, she saw no hint of amusement or knowledge of the double entendre and she just said, 'Sure.' Anna felt quite safe with him now, having realised intuitively that, despite his obvious flirting skills, he wouldn't dare take things any further than just that – flirting. He really was basically shy around girls.

So they left the kitchen together and went to his room where he took out CD after CD, explaining a little about each of the artists as he did so. Then he put on one of Duke Ellington and they listened in silence for a bit, sitting on the floor. Anna was once again struck by its complex rhythmic harmonies and told Graham this. He chuckled and said, 'Wait till you hear some of the more modern stuff I have. But I think it's better for you to start with the standard classics before we move onto that. Did you know that the majority of modern jazz artists have been classically trained?'

'No, I didn't,' she admitted and then asked a question of her own. 'Has jazz ever fused with other music forms?'

'At one time or another it's fused with just about every musical form known to man,' Graham replied. 'But I think it's always managed to be instantly recognisable.'

'Now I come to think of it, I've heard it on various pop records too,' Anna said thoughtfully.

'I'm sure you have. Today jazz rhythms are becoming more and more popular with pop people.'

'Do you play an instrument yourself?' Anna asked.

'Not really. I bang away sometimes on the piano. How about you?' he replied.

'I used to have piano lessons but gave up. My teacher was a real dragon.'

While they were talking, Anna had been trying to think of a way to change the subject and ask Graham what she thought was a good question. But she couldn't really think of a tactful one so she decided just to come straight out with it.

'Graham,' she said hesitantly during a pause in the conversation. 'Why do you call your dad Peter and not Dad like everyone else I know?'

Graham looked at her closely and then said, equally hesitantly, 'Wow! That's quite a change of subject. Well, my real dad died when I was a baby in a flying accident. I never knew him. Mum was absolutely devastated for seven years. She couldn't even work then. Then she pulled herself out of it and, when I was eight, she met Peter and married him. He was divorced but had no children of his own.'

Anna looked at him with her mouth open in astonishment. 'So Peter's your *step*-dad!' she exclaimed.

'Yes, but to me he's much more real than my real one.'

'I guess you must've had a pretty miserable childhood?'

'Yes. We had little money and I was a real handful. That was why I was so pleased when Peter came along. He took charge of me and it was exactly what I needed.'

'He and your mum seem so happy together. They don't

appear to have the same arguments as in every other family I know.'

'It's true. They are very happy together and I'm so pleased to now have a father figure in my life. Sure they argue, often about me, but I think Mum's terrified of losing him so she never pushes it too far.'

'Thank you for sharing that with me,' Anna said humbly.

'Since we've got onto personal stuff, can you tell me anything about *your* dad?' Graham asked her now.

'I only know what Mum's told me, which isn't much. I suspect it's rather a censored version of events. Apparently he was a charming rogue, always flirting with other women, and, when I was four, he ran off with a younger version of my mum. As far as I know, he doesn't even pay maintenance for me. That's how little contact Mum has with him. The only thing he left her was the house with a twenty-year mortgage to pay off.'

'Have you ever seen a picture of him?'

'I can't remember ever seeing one. I think Mum must've destroyed them all when he left.'

'I guess that explains why there are no pictures of you as a baby in your house. He must've been holding you in all of them.'

'I guess so,' Anna replied.

'And has your mum ever had a boyfriend since?' he persisted.

'If she has, she's never told me about him,' Anna said.

They both sat there then, listening to the Duke burbling away in the background and thinking that here was something important they both shared, having no real father around.

Finally, Anna got to her feet and said, 'I think that's enough personal revelations for one night, don't you? I'm going to bed.' So after saying goodnight and getting a friendly wave from Graham, she left him.

She lay on her bed for a while, thinking about what he'd said, then slowly got undressed, washed and got into bed. She tried to read but couldn't concentrate so she put the book down. Her last thought before going to sleep was not about her mother but about how pleased she was that Graham trusted her enough to tell her about his family background. She slept better than she had the night before but woke up early again on Tuesday morning. Looking out of the window, she noticed that the sky was grey and cloudy, promising rain later.

Chapter 13

Tuesday followed much the same pattern as Monday. Anna went to the hospital again in the morning, sat by her mother's bed and told her all about the homework she'd done the previous afternoon, the book she'd just started and the conversation she'd had with Graham before she went to bed. At one point she said, 'When you wake up, Mum, you're going to have to tell me more about my dad, such as is there any way of contacting him, not that I want to at the moment but I might do one day.' But there was still no reaction from her mother.

She left the hospital and was home by lunchtime where she met Peter cooking again. 'How did it go?' he asked.

'No change,' Anna replied.

'Did you have an interesting chat to Graham last night?' he asked then.

She looked at him, wondering if Graham had talked to him about the conversation they'd had but there was only genuine curiosity in his eyes. So she just said, 'Yes, very. He began introducing me properly to jazz. I enjoyed it.'

'Good,' was all he said.

After lunch she went back to her room and continued to do school work until Graham came back. They chatted for a while until he disappeared to do his own homework while Anna continued to read her book.

After supper Graham had more to do and Gemma asked Anna if she fancied watching TV. Anna said yes so they went into the small cosy front lounge and sat companionably together on the sofa, watching one of Anna's favourite TV shows which, it turned out, was also one of Gemma's favourites. It was a period drama set in the 19th century and, after it was over they discussed why they both liked it which brought them even closer together. When the news came on at ten o'clock, Anna yawned and said, 'I guess I'm sleepy. I think I'll go on up.'

'Sweet dreams, Anna. It's been really nice for me to be able to watch the TV during the week with somebody for a change,' Gemma said.

So Anna went upstairs and prepared for bed. There she read a bit more, turned the light out and went to sleep, feeling safe and warm. She had no more nightmares although her last thoughts were about her mother.

The rest of that week was pretty similar, the only variation in what Anna did being on the Wednesday when she popped in at her house after the hospital to check the answer phone for messages. There was only one from Serena saying that she'd been in to visit her mum the afternoon before and how depressed she'd felt when she left. Anna didn't bother replying and, as soon as she'd checked the fridge and thrown out a few things that were well past their sell-by date and beginning to smell, she left the house without seeing Mrs Carrington and cycled home.

Then on Friday evening Gemma reminded her quietly that

tomorrow was Saturday, the day of the memorial service, and asked her if she still wanted to go. 'Yes, I'd like to very much,' Anna replied. Gemma sighed and said, 'OK. We'll leave about 9.30. I've checked the arrangements and we should arrive at the cathedral shortly before the cortege gets there.'

'OK. Thanks a lot, Gemma,' Anna said and went to bed.

Chapter 14

When she woke up, she looked out of the window and noticed that the sky was grey and dreary. A suitable day for a memorial service, she thought grimly. Then she knew she had to decide what to wear. So, after washing, she looked through the few clothes she had brought with her but couldn't find anything in black, which she supposed was the appropriate colour for a memorial service. She'd never been to one before and had no idea what to expect. So she just pulled on a dark blue T-shirt, which fortunately had no writing on it. But then she remembered her school uniform, which was grey, and she decided to wear that over the top. So she put on her school skirt and black school shoes and finally her school jacket which mostly covered up the T-shirt. She checked her appearance in the big mirror on the wardrobe door and was satisfied she looked suitably sober.

Then she went downstairs to the kitchen. Gemma was there, dressed in dark colours herself, and she gave Anna an approving look before she sat down and started her breakfast. 'Do I look OK?' Anna asked anxiously. 'You look fine. It was a good idea to wear your uniform,' Gemma said and Anna was relieved. It was nearly 9 o'clock by the time she'd finished breakfast and cleared everything away and neither Graham nor Peter had appeared yet.

So she went back upstairs and tidied her room. Finally she checked her mobile and put it in her jacket pocket. She'd decided not to take her rucksack as she didn't really need it. Then, with one final pull of a comb through her hair, she put a couple of hair grips in and checked her appearance again. She'd do, she thought grimly. Then she looked at her watch, saw that it was nearly 9.30 and ran back downstairs.

She met Gemma in the hall and they went out together to the car.

'I understand the streets around the cathedral itself have been sealed off. I guess they're expecting a big crowd. So I'll have to park a little distance away and we'll walk from there,' Gemma said.

'OK,' Anna replied distractedly.

They set off and, as they got closer to the city centre, they saw many people, all walking sombrely and quietly towards the cathedral. Gemma was looking for somewhere to park and she finally managed to squeeze the car between two others on a side street. They got out and joined the crowd.

When they got to the huge square in front of the cathedral, it was to find it absolutely packed, a jostling sea of humanity. Anna looked over the heads of a party of school children in front of her and noticed that a massive screen, showing the inside of the cathedral, which was similarly crowded, had been put up outside with enormous speakers flanking it although these were still silent. There were many police around but, as far as Anna could see, everybody was well-behaved and they didn't seem necessary. She looked at her watch. 9.55.

Then there was a noise from the crowd behind her and she turned to see a long cavalcade of big, black hearses with coffins inside making its way slowly through the crowd towards the front of the cathedral. Anna counted twelve of them. Next she saw a large number of men and women in uniform, who seemed to be firemen, policemen and paramedics, lining up on the steps, forming a guard of honour. She wondered if they had been the first on the scene that awful morning. After that she saw the coffins being taken out of the hearses by a number of burly men, four to each coffin, and carried slowly and carefully up the steps and into the cathedral. She looked at the screen where the speakers had suddenly blared into life. The congregation inside were singing a hymn to the accompaniment of the organ, one she thought she recognised. The coffins were all laid out in front of the altar in two rows of six. The pictures were so pin sharp as the camera slowly panned across the faces of the people inside, lingering longest on the faces of the famous, that she could even see the tears glistening on some of the women's cheeks.

Suddenly she spotted the girl with the red hair she'd seen in the waiting room of the hospital who'd been crying. She was sitting in the second row of pews and was still crying as if she hadn't stopped since last Friday. So she *had* lost somebody, Anna thought sadly. Was it her mum? She was sitting next to the same man she'd seen so fleetingly the previous week. He had tears leaking out from beneath his closed eyes but no longer had his arms around her. She wished she could comfort them both. But what could she possibly say?

But she didn't see them again for then the camera stopped panning and came to rest on a man at the front. He was dressed imposingly in a long, white robe covered by what to her inexperienced church-goer's eyes looked like a kind of purple cloak with slits down the sides. She presumed it was the bishop. After the hymn everybody fell silent for a few moments of contemplative prayer and then the bishop started talking.

He began by welcoming everybody who'd managed to turn out at the service and then said, 'We are gathered here today for the sad task of saying goodbye to some of our own whose lives were cut short so tragically just over a week ago.' Then he went on to describe the unutterable loss felt by the victims' families. He continued by reminding everybody of the families of those whose loved ones had been injured in the blast, saying that the congregation should pray for them too. That brought tears to Anna's eyes. And he concluded by stating that no one would ever really understand how anybody could do such a thing and that, while he felt the people's anger at the perpetrators, he hoped that nobody would try to take the law into their own hands. After all, he said, the city had lived peacefully together as a multi-cultural melting-pot for many years. Anna, who had assiduously avoided watching or listening to the news since that first time on the radio with Gemma, wondered why he had included this and knew she would have to find out more about the bombing. But there was a murmur from the crowd outside at his words and Anna could almost feel the waves of anger physically battering her mind like they'd done when she'd first heard about the bombing on the radio. It's all very well for you to say, she thought bitterly. I bet you never lost anybody to anything like this. But then she reflected that all in all it had been a good sermon and not too long. The bishop had been inclusive in his comments and at least had never once mentioned forgiving the terrorists for their wicked act.

Then the organ struck up again and another hymn was sung, this time by the choir alone, while the bishop went slowly around the coffins sprinkling them with what Anna presumed was holy water. Somebody read out the names of the victims and finally a couple more hymns were sung this time by everybody who knew the words both inside and outside the cathedral, which Anna found very moving. Finally the huge doors of the church were flung open and the coffins were carried out by the same groups of men she had seen bringing them in. They were reverentially put back in the hearses which then drove off, Anna presumed, either to be buried or cremated by their families. The huge crowd threw bunches of flowers at the departing cars until the whole square seemed to be awash with them.

As the crowd slowly left the square, Anna turned to Gemma who'd been standing beside her silently the whole time and said, 'I'd like to go into the cathedral for a few moments if that's OK.' Gemma looked at her closely, wondering probably if she was going to break down, but Anna was dry-eyed. They passed through the crowd and up the steps and through the doors into the vast, open space inside with its impossibly high roof. The cathedral was emptying fast now and Anna saw the TV crews all packing away their equipment. She spotted a few famous faces, including that of the Prime Minister who was talking quietly to the bishop near the altar surrounded by a number of tough-looking guys, who she presumed were his bodyguards. It occurred to her briefly that the powerful had to put up with the threat of sudden violence for a lot of their working lives and she wondered how they coped. But he wasn't why she was there. She just wanted to say a quick prayer for her mother and all the other victims. So she sat down in one of the empty pews and laid her head on the hard back of the pew in front. Haltingly she said her prayer, helped by the hushed atmosphere, and afterwards she felt better. She didn't understand why that should be but was glad she'd done it. Then she joined Gemma who'd been standing patiently at the back and they left the cathedral in silence.

They didn't talk until they were back at the car when Anna turned to Gemma and said, 'Thank you for taking me, Gemma. It was important to me.'

Gemma smiled at her and said, 'Not at all. It was my pleasure. Do you want to go straight home or go by the hospital?'

'I think I'd rather go to the hospital this afternoon. I have a lot to think about.'

'It was a big turnout, wasn't it?'

'Yes, much bigger than I thought it would be,' Anna replied. 'I hadn't realised that the shock had been felt by so many people.'

'I thought the bishop's sermon struck the right note.'

'Yes, I agree.' And those were the last words they exchanged until they got home.

Anna looked up at the sky as they arrived home and saw the sun struggling fitfully to break through the cloud cover. Maybe it'll be a nice afternoon, she thought. She went straight up to her room, took her still-silent mobile out of her pocket and put it on her desk. Then she changed out of her school uniform and put her jeans on. She felt restless and decided she needed to speak to Graham. So, going along to his room, she knocked timidly. She heard his voice ask her to come in and she was greeted by a beaming Graham who seemed genuinely pleased to see her. He was sitting on the floor, surrounded by sundry bits of computer. But it looked more complete than it'd done the last time she'd seen it. 'How was the ceremony?' he asked.

'Very big and grand,' she replied. 'I'm sure it'll be all over the TV. I saw the Prime Minister.'

'Really?' Graham said, seeming impressed.

'What've you been up to?' she asked, changing the subject.

'As you can see, I'm still trying to put this blasted computer together but I'm making good progress. It's actually a part of a school project.'

'Are you going for a swim this afternoon?'

'Yes, probably. Do you want to come?'

'Yes, I'd like to but first I'd like to go by the hospital. Can you wait for me?'

'Sure. As long as you're not too long.'

'I'm not planning on a long visit today.'

'OK. That's settled then. I'm hungry. Let's go down and see if lunch is ready.'

In the event it wasn't quite ready so they both went outside and Graham pumped up one of Anna's tyres which seemed a bit low. After he'd done that, they went for a stroll round the garden in the sunshine and Graham chattered on to her about the various things he was involved in at school. She was trying to make some sense of everything she'd seen that morning and was quite happy just to listen to him, only putting in the occasional word to keep the flow going.

Then they were called in and Graham was asked to go and get Peter. They all sat down and had a proper lunch and Anna found that surprisingly she was hungry. They talked a bit about the service and Anna asked why the bishop had warned people against taking the law into their own hands. Peter and Gemma both looked at her closely when she asked this, obviously pleased that she could at last talk about the bombing openly.

'Because an Islamic fundamentalist group has claimed responsibility and clearly we don't want a race war here,' Peter replied quietly.

'Oh,' was all Anna could find to say, thinking of her Muslim classmates at school who, as a group, were probably the nicest people she knew. Then, realising that she now needed to pay proper attention to the news, she asked, 'Have they found any other terrorists yet?'

'They've arrested a couple of people but haven't charged them yet,' Peter replied again. And there Anna dropped the subject.

When they'd finished eating, Peter said, 'Thanks for that, Gemma. It filled a hole. It's back to the salt mine for me,' and he left the table. Anna realised that, like her mother who was also self-employed, he could rarely take time off work.

She helped Gemma tidy up and then went upstairs and

fetched her mobile, looking at it quickly. There was a message from the hospital. Opening it, she saw that it said, 'Come quickly. We think your mother's starting to wake up!' Hyper-excited now, she rushed back downstairs, went outside to the bike and pedalled away as fast as she could to the hospital without even passing on the news to the family.

Chapter 15

She got there in record time, raced up to the ward and was almost at once greeted by a nurse she recognised with an 'Oh, there you are. Come along quickly.' She ran down the corridor and barged into her mother's room without bothering with the mask and gown. There were a number of nurses clustered around her Mum's bed and she thought she felt a feeling of excitement in the air. She looked at the brain activity monitor and saw that it was no longer a flat line with the occasional blip but was spiking madly, the lines going up and down in an irregular rhythm.

'Is it true she's waking up?' she demanded frantically.

The duty ward sister, who she knew by sight, turned to her and said, 'Thanks for coming. Yes, we think so.'

'That's fantastic!' Anna said, still in shock over the possibility.

'We'll leave you alone for a bit,' the sister said, handing her a new mask and gown. 'Call us at once using the red button if you see any change.'

Anna promised she would and, putting on the mask and gown, sat down by the bed, waiting for the nurses to file out. She looked closely at her mother now and saw her eyelids flickering but they still remained shut. She hoped against hope that the nurses were right and it wasn't just another false alarm. She held her mum's hand as she had done so often recently and started telling her about the memorial service she'd been to that morning. She was well into her recitation when her mother's eyes suddenly opened fully and she stared at her daughter. Her mouth opened and she seemed to be trying to speak. Could this really be the moment Anna had been waiting for so desperately?

'Hello, Mum, are you awake at last?' she said, hardly daring to believe what was happening.

'Anna, is that you?' her mother croaked in a voice unused to speaking and sounding muffled through the mask. 'Where am I? What happened? Why are you wearing that mask?' Anna was so pleased her mother was finally talking that she burst into tears and couldn't reply to her questions. She felt the pressure on her hand increase as her mother gripped her hand more tightly. 'What's the matter, darling? Please don't cry,' she said now. Anna dried the tears with the back of her hand and pressed the red button.

The ward sister arrived almost immediately with a couple of nurses in tow and, seeing her mother's eyes open, immediately quizzed Anna about what had happened. Anna told her briefly and she nodded in satisfaction saying, 'That's very good news. I must call a doctor,' and she pressed a button on the pager attached to her belt.

Meanwhile her mother had continued staring at Anna with a look of terror on her face. 'Am I in hospital?' she croaked now and then asked, 'What's the matter with my voice?'

'Sssh, Mum. Just lie quietly,' Anna said. One of the nurses had taken off her oxygen mask and was giving her some water to drink and, although most of it seemed to dribble down her chin, she did manage to swallow some. Then Anna said, 'Yes, Mum. You're in hospital. You had an accident and got a bad bump on your head.'

'Oh,' her mother said simply. Then she asked in a slightly stronger voice, 'How long have I been here?'

'Just over a week, Mum,' Anna replied.

'What? Oh, no! That's impossible!'

'I'm afraid it's true, Mum,' Anna said. And her mother closed her eyes and said nothing more for a bit.

Then a doctor arrived, an Indian one by his looks and accent, and asked the ward sister a lot of questions but Anna wasn't listening to him. She was staring at what she could see of her mother's pale face. Finally the doctor seemed satisfied with the answers he'd got and asked Anna if she'd mind leaving the room while he examined her. She did so and paced nervously up and down the corridor outside. Then she thought to ring Gemma. She picked up quickly and Anna gave her the news, almost bursting into tears again.

'Good,' she said. 'I'm coming over to the hospital now. Wait there.'

'Thanks, Gemma,' Anna said weakly. 'Can you tell Graham that our swimming expedition will have to be postponed?'

'Sure,' Gemma said and Anna hung up.

Then the doctor came out and spoke to Gemma outside. He said, 'Well, it seems that no damage has been done to your mother's speech centres which was something we were all worried about but I'm afraid there is no reaction from the right side of her body. We'll just have to wait and see how that develops.'

'Do you mean the right side of her body is paralysed?' Anna asked with horror.

'At the moment, yes, I'm afraid so but there is every chance she'll recover fully,' he replied.

'Oh,' was all Anna could find to say. When they went back into her room, her mother's eyes were fully open and she looked even more terrified if that was possible without the oxygen mask on now. The doctor patted her shoulder and said, 'Try not to worry, Mrs Sixsmith. We're going to make you better.' Then he left.

'Can I be left alone with my daughter, please?' her mother said. 'We obviously have a lot of catching up to do.'

'Yes, of course,' the ward sister said and, after telling her mother not to tire herself and Anna to give her water if she wanted it, she and the nurses left. She added, 'Oh, and don't worry about the Barrier Nursing procedures now.'

Anna thanked her and, taking off the uncomfortable mask and the gown, sat down beside the bed. 'What kind of accident did I have?' her mother asked her.

Anna was still thinking through the implications of paralysis and wasn't concentrating on her mum's question. She wasn't sure whether the doctor had told her about it and resolved not to mention it first. So she had to ask her mother to repeat the question. But when she'd done so, Anna didn't know whether to tell her the truth or not. All these secrets, she thought despondently. But she compromised by telling her a half-truth. 'There was an explosion in the city while you were at work and you got caught up in it.' That seemed to satisfy her mother and she asked a few more, less difficult questions before her eyelids started drooping and she quickly dropped off to sleep again while Anna was still speaking.

Then Gemma appeared, panting slightly, and said, 'I got here as quickly as I could.' She looked at the brain monitoring machine and said, 'Well, your mother seems to be sleeping normally now. That's very good.' Anna told her what the doctor had said about the lack of reaction on the right side of her body and Gemma frowned and said, 'Well, clearly she's going to need a lot of physiotherapy as she gets better but that's to be expected.'

'When do you think she'll be able to come home?'

'That's up to Mr Penny to decide. He'll be visiting her on Monday morning. But I don't expect it'll be for quite a while yet.'

'Oh,' Anna said dejectedly. 'I was hoping that, after she woke up, she'd be able to come home almost immediately.'

'I'm afraid it's going to be quite a long process, Anna,' Gemma said gently.

Anna felt emotionally wrung out and asked, 'Can I sleep in here with her?'

'Yes, I don't see why not,' Gemma said. 'Wait here.' And she disappeared. When she returned some time later, she had a porter with her who was wheeling a collapsible bed. He quickly set it up and left.

''Thank you, Gemma,' Anna said.

'I arranged everything with the ward sister on duty. You should be fine. But don't expect to get much sleep. You know how often people have to come in and check things. Also this can't be a permanent solution. It'll only be for tonight. Then you'll have to come home.'

'OK,' Anna said, willingly surrendering all responsibility to the older woman.

'Have you got any money with you? You'll need to eat later.'

Anna felt in her pocket and produced the note she had put in there for emergencies. 'Yes, thanks.'

'I'll leave you now and come back again tomorrow morning. By the way, both Peter and Graham were delighted with the news.' And she left too, leaving Anna alone with her sleeping mother.

She lay down fully-dressed on the small bed after closing the blinds on the window and quite quickly fell into a fitful sleep. She was used by now to the machines bleeping away around her mum but she was still partially woken up several times by nurses coming in to check on her mother but they didn't make much noise and she soon dropped off again.

When she finally woke properly, she was groggy and disorientated, having no idea where she was or what time it was. The room was dark and silent. But then it all came rushing back to her and she got up unsteadily, stumbling over some of the wires leading into her mother as she did so but without waking her. She went outside into the corridor and looked at her watch. It was 9 pm already. She had slept most of the afternoon and evening away. She knew she had to find a toilet so she wandered down the corridor until she saw a door with the familiar image on it. She had a pee and then washed her face and hands thoroughly in cold water until she was properly awake again.

She felt hungry now and told the nurse on duty at the desk that she was going down in the lift to find a canteen. Everything she needed was in the main concourse and she bought herself a large hamburger and a soft drink which she finished quickly, sitting at a table by herself. Then she thought she ought to get some toothpaste if she was going to stay the night so she found a small supermarket selling everything from sandwiches to shaving cream for men. She got the toothpaste there and then went back up to the ward. The nurse smiled at her as she entered and told her that her Mum was still sleeping soundly and added that it was a good sign. Anna smiled back at her and walked slowly back to her mother's room.

She lay down again fully clothed in the darkened room and tried to sleep. But this time she found she couldn't and she started thinking about the events of the day. Was it her prayer in the cathedral that had woken up her mum? Not that she cared. She just felt happy they were going to be able to communicate again. Then she considered the possibility that maybe her Mum would never be able to walk again but would remain paralysed and be confined to a wheelchair. That was the worst scenario that she could imagine. But then she thought that millions of people seemed to be able to function adequately with some help even if they were in a wheelchair.

She was absolutely determined that she was going to be 'the primary carer' during her recovery, a phrase she'd heard somewhere. But she also reckoned that she should be able to get some help from the government so that her education would not be too badly disrupted. After all her mum had paid her taxes all her life and surely was entitled to get something back. All these thoughts went whizzing through her mind and, as they were mostly positive, she decided that she didn't have too much to worry about at present. It'd take the hospital as long as it took to release her mum and, it was true, she was in good hands here.

She finally managed to fall asleep again, still fully clothed, although she was disturbed several times in the night as Gemma had predicted.

Chapter 16

When she woke up, the early morning sun was shining through the blinds and Anna got up quickly, feeling rather tired. She looked at her mum but there seemed to be no change. She was still sleeping peacefully. She went to the toilet, washed her face and hands and swilled some toothpaste around her mouth. That made her feel cleaner although she knew she had to change her clothes but they'd have to wait. Then she popped down to the canteen and had a quick bite to eat before rushing back to the ward.

There she found the same Indian doctor and a couple of new nurses scrutinising her Mum's medical chart. 'I'm glad you're here,' he said. 'We're just about to wake her up. Could you try talking to her?'

So Anna sat beside her bed and, squeezing her left hand, said, 'Mum, it's me. Can you hear me?'

There was a little twitch of her mother's fingers and then she opened her eyes and smiled when she saw Anna. 'Why, Anna, you're still here!' she exclaimed.

'Yes. I've been here all night.'

'Oh, thank you, darling! But you really shouldn't have bothered, you know. I had some lovely dreams.....I think.'

'Good. I'm glad, Mum,' Anna said. 'The doctor's here.'

Then he broke in saying, 'Mrs Sixsmith. My name is Dr Venju. Perhaps you remember me from yesterday. I'm the registrar on the ward at the moment. We're going to sit you up.' And the nurses hurried to do his bidding. 'We'd like you to try eating something by yourself. Do you think you could manage that?'

'I'm not sure. I think so but I don't really feel hungry.'

One of the nurses then produced a bowl of what looked like porridge and a napkin and proceeded to spoon very small quantities of it into her mouth. She dribbled most of it down her chin where the napkin caught it but managed to swallow a little. The doctor, who'd been watching with approval, said when the nurse looked enquiringly at him, 'Good. That'll do for now. We shouldn't need to keep you on the intravenous feeding drip for much longer.'

Anna's mother smiled at him and said, 'I guess I'm happy about that if you are.' And Anna felt a rush of love for her. She was being so brave.

Then the doctor said, 'You need to get plenty of rest. We'll leave you alone now with your daughter,' adding as he looked at Anna, 'Don't tire her out, will you?'

'No, doctor,' Anna replied meekly as they left.

'I remember you talking to me - Was it yesterday? But I can't remember any details. Did I fall asleep?'

'Yes,' Anna said, 'Would you like me to start again?'

'Yes, please, darling. By the way, your spots seem to have almost disappeared. You look pretty.'

Anna laughed and said, 'I know. Thanks, Mum.' Then, not mentioning her accident or the funerals which she'd been telling her about the previous day, she recounted the whole story of the Frost family and how she'd come to stay with them and this time her mother didn't fall asleep but listened intently to every word.

When she stopped, her mum said, 'Well, you really seem to have fallen on your feet with them. I'm very glad for you, darling.'

'You should have the chance to meet Gemma today. She's coming in. Last night she told me I couldn't stay with you more than one night.'

'That'll be nice. I'd like to thank her for looking after you. And of course you can't stay here permanently. You know I'll be fine.'

They talked some more, Anna telling her about their own house and how she had rung Serena and Miriam and her two clients and she finally said that Serena had come in to visit her some days earlier. Then she stopped again and her mother commented, 'My, how grown up you've been! I'm so proud of you.'

At that moment there was a knock on the door and Gemma came in, dressed in her normal clothes, not her nurse's uniform. She smiled and said, 'Hello, Anna. Hello, Mrs Sixsmith. I'm Mrs Frost but I hope you'll call me Gemma. It's very good indeed to see you awake. Has Anna mentioned me?'

'You and your delightful family are almost all she's talked about. Thank you ever so much for having her. Oh and by the way, please call me Pauline.'

'OK, Pauline. It's no problem at all having Anna stay. It's actually very nice for me to have a girl around who can help out and who I can have a natter to. I just popped in to see how you were getting on and to ask Anna if she wanted a lift home yet. I'll see you tomorrow in my official capacity.'

'I was hoping to go home soon,' Anna's mother said.

'Mr Penny, your consultant, will be coming in to see you tomorrow and, as I told Anna yesterday, he'll talk to you about that.' While she said this, Gemma was studying her medical chart. Now she turned around and continued, 'Well, it looks as if you're recovering well but you still have a way to go.'

'OK,' Anna's mum said. 'You run along now, Anna. All this talk and excitement seem to have made me feel sleepy again.'

'Is there anything you'd like Anna to bring you from home?' Gemma asked now.

She considered this question and then said, 'No, not just at the moment. When I'm feeling stronger, there will be things I need, like my night clothes and washing things, but I'm fine for the moment.'

'OK, Mum,' Anna said. 'I'll see you tomorrow morning and we'll have a proper chat with Mr Penny. You get some rest now,' and she kissed her mother and left the room with Gemma.

As they were going back down in the lift, Anna asked Gemma what problems there might be with her mother coming home. Gemma looked at her closely and, in a sad tone, replied by asking her if she remembered what Dr Venju had said about the lack of response from the right side of her body

'Yes. I remember it well. But so what? She could use a wheelchair, couldn't she?' Anna said.

'Well,' Gemma continued slowly. 'One thing is that your Mum is going to need more or less full-time professional help for quite a while even after the physiotherapy starts to work and I'm afraid you're not qualified to provide that. So that will have to be set up as a priority and it can take a while. Then some changes will have to be made to your house to help her get around. All these things take time. I doubt if she's even aware yet that the right side of her body's paralysed. That's something Mr Penny will have to discuss with her.'

'Oh,' she replied dejectedly, although she was pleased she'd decided not to mention the paralysis to her mum before Mr Penny did.

They'd got to Gemma's car when Anna suddenly remembered she'd arrived on the bike and mentioned it to Gemma.

'Don't worry about it. It'll be quite safe here,' she said.

'But you leave so early in the morning. How am I going to get to the hospital with neither the bike nor your car?' Anna said.

'I hadn't thought of that,' Gemma admitted. 'OK. You take the bike home. I'll be waiting for you.'

'OK and thanks for coming in, Gemma.' But she waved away her thanks and Anna turned back to get the bike. She pedalled home quickly as there was little traffic around, it being a Sunday again. When she got there, she found Gemma in the kitchen, preparing lunch. 'I'll go upstairs and have a shower and change,' she told her.

'Fine,' Gemma said.

When she came down feeling clean again, she was carrying a large pile of dirty clothes. 'Just shove them in the washing machine. I'll do them later,' Gemma told her. So Anna did that and then started to help by laying the table. While she was doing this, Gemma turned to Anna and said, 'I meant what I said to your mother. It really is very nice for me to have you around. I'll miss you when you go home.' And when Anna looked at her closely, she could see tears glistening in her eyes.

'This will always be my second home now,' Anna said and she gave Gemma a big hug and got an even bigger one back. It made them both feel better. Gemma now asked her to call the guys as lunch was ready and, as usual, she found Peter in his office and Graham in his room. Graham jumped up from his chair when she came in and said excitedly, 'I'm really glad your mum's woken up and that you're back. Is it lunchtime? Would you like to go swimming this afternoon? I postponed my swimming yesterday in the hope that you would.'

'Yes, to both questions,' Anna said, smiling at him. She'd been looking forward to the prospect of getting some decent exercise after being cooped up in the hospital for so long.

'That's great,' Graham said.

When they had all assembled in the kitchen, Peter asked Anna for a blow-by-blow account of her stay at the hospital and she obliged but omitted any details of the roller-coaster of emotions she'd been through, sticking just to the facts. After lunch she went upstairs again, got her swimming stuff and met Graham coming out of his bedroom carrying his own rucksack. 'Ready?' he asked. 'Yes. Let's go,' she replied. And they cycled together back to his school.

That day they had the pool entirely to themselves, which to Anna was extraordinary. They had a couple more races but the results were the same as the week before. Although Graham offered to show her more of the school, she declined and they cycled home.

On the way back, Anna thought about Graham. She knew she enjoyed being with him, in spite of the enormous differences in their backgrounds, and was attracted to him. However, she wasn't sure if the relationship was destined to remain that of brother and sister like it seemed to be now or if it might become something more. But she made a resolution. Nothing would happen while she was living under the same roof as him. It would feel incestuous. Later she would see. She had never had a proper boyfriend but she knew she was more worldly-wise than he was and had already decided that Graham was too inexperienced with girls to take the first step if their relationship was destined to develop into something else. She'd have to do it herself.

They had tea together, then went up to Graham's room where they played with his train set, staging an exciting crash. After that she excused herself on the grounds of tiredness and went back to her own room where she found her laundry piled onto her bed, washed, ironed and neatly folded. Then she had a nap, something unusual for her normally, but she knew she hadn't had enough sleep the night before and the exercise she'd had that afternoon had made her tired. After she'd woken up, she saw that it was nearly suppertime and went down to help Gemma in the kitchen and thanked her for doing her laundry. They all had supper together and afterwards she watched TV with Gemma until the news had finished. It was still dominated by reports of the outrage and Anna watched with interest now. She talked about it a bit with Gemma and then went up to bed, feeling reasonably happy for the first time for what seemed like ages.

CHAPTER 17

The next day Anna woke up quite early and went down to the kitchen, finding both Graham and Peter there, Graham, as usual on a weekday, dressed in his school uniform. They both grunted 'Hi' through mouthfuls of cereal and she made her own breakfast but, before she'd finished, Graham dumped his dirty bowl and coffee cup in the sink and said, 'Right. I'm off. See you later,' and left.

Peter, who by now had finished eating, looked directly at Anna and said, 'So today you've got an important interview with your mum's consultant. Is that right?'

Anna hesitated, then said, 'I'm not sure if he's going to be able to tell me anything I don't already know.'

'Anyway, I think it might be wise to make a list of the questions you want to ask him.'

'Yes, that's a very good idea, Peter. I'll certainly do that.'

'I always find it useful to make lists. Otherwise I know I'll forget something important.'

'Yes, I have to do the same usually,' Anna said. Then Peter left the kitchen to do his mysterious work and Anna put everything away in the dishwasher and tidied the kitchen. After that she went back to her room and started compiling the list of questions for Mr Penny but she didn't get very far as the most important question for her was 'When can my mother come home?' She knew he would probably reply with something like, 'It depends,' or 'How long is a piece of string?' Still, never mind. She did, however, manage to think of a few more things she wanted to ask and she put the list in her pocket before getting her rucksack and making sure she had everything she needed. Then she left her room, went downstairs and outside and got her bike. She was forced to cycle more slowly than the day before because of the traffic and it was 9.30 by the time she got to the hospital.

She went inside after locking her bike and up to her mother's ward. She was buzzed in as usual and walked down the corridor to her mother's room. She peered inside and was relieved to see her mother alone, propped up in bed and listening to something through headphones over the top of her white turban with a beatific smile on her face. They were attached to a device which from the back looked like some sort of screen. Anna went in and her mother took the headphones off with her left hand and gave Anna a big smile. 'Hello, darling,' she said.

'Hello, Mum,' Anna replied. 'Have you seen Mr Penny yet?'

'No, not yet. But I'm expecting him very soon. So one of the lovely nurses told me anyway. I've been listening to Radio 2. They've been playing some of my favourite music. It's all free, you know, the radio, but you have to pay for the TV and phone,' she said, gesturing to the machine in front of her with her left hand. Anna had been looking at it and noticed now that it had a long bendable arm. It must've been swung up high which was why she hadn't noticed it before.

'That's nice, Mum. If you want to watch TV or make a

phone call, I can give you the money. Gemma has given me plenty.'

'She really is extraordinarily kind, isn't she? But that won't be necessary. It's all done by credit card and I assume mine's here still in my handbag. I saw her earlier, by the way. She looked quite intimidating in her uniform. But she seems like a lovely person.'

'She is, Mum. She really is.'

Then her mother changed the subject to one Anna had been fearing. She said, 'I was listening to the news on Radio 2 a little while ago and they said something about a terrorist explosion in the city over a week ago. That wouldn't have been the explosion I was caught up in, would it?'

Anna knew she had to tell the truth now and said simply, 'Yes, Mum. That was it.'

'How truly dreadful,' her mother replied.

But that was as far as the conversation went for now because Mr Penny came in, alone this time. 'Hello, Miss Sixsmith,' he said. And then to her mother, 'My name's Mr Penny. How are you feeling, Mrs Sixsmith?' he said.

'Much better, thank you, doctor. Anna and I have been waiting to have a chat with you.'

'And so you will. But first I have to examine you. I'm just waiting for Mrs Frost to assist me. She should be here any moment.'

Just then Gemma came bustling in and said, 'Sorry, doctor. I got held up. Hi, Anna. Hi, Pauline.'

'Would you mind waiting outside?' Mr Penny asked Anna. She was used to this by now and didn't resent it. So she went into the corridor, took a folding chair from the waiting room, sat down and pulled out the list of questions for the doctor. She read it through and a couple more occurred to her, which she added with a pen she took from her rucksack. After what seemed like an interminable wait but was probably no more than ten minutes, Gemma poked her head round the door and called Anna. She followed her back into the room and she saw her mother looking very pale as if she'd had some kind of shock.

'Oh, darling!' her mum exclaimed. 'I've just found out that I can't move my right arm or leg! It's like I've had some kind of stroke!' She looked as if she might burst into tears and Anna went up to her and gripped her left hand tightly.

'That's exactly what you've had, Mrs Sixsmith,' Mr Penny said in a kindly voice, not his usual peremptory bark. 'A kind of stroke induced by the trauma of your injury. I've explained to your mother, Miss Sixsmith, that people have recovered fully from worse injuries than this. Once the brain has rewired itself, your mother should be as good as new. I'm very pleased with her progress so far. She's starting to take solid food now and I think the drip feed should be able to be removed by the end of the day.' Here he paused, then asked, 'Any questions so far?'

Her mum looked at him and asked what for Anna and her was the most important question of all. 'When will I be able to go home, doctor?'

'You need to be kept an eye on here for a while but, basically, as soon as the necessary support is in place. That usually takes from six to eight weeks. I'll set the whole thing in motion today.'

Six to eight weeks! Anna was appalled but at least now

she had some kind of time frame to work within. Her mother anxiously asked another question now. 'Will I have to pay for it?'

'No. It's all free on the NHS,' he replied.

'That's a relief,' she said.

'Anything else?'

Anna pulled out the list of questions she'd made and asked them. Mr Penny dealt with them all quickly and efficiently and to Anna's satisfaction. He even managed to make the medical language understandable to her by paraphrasing any difficult words he used.

'OK. Thank you very much for everything, doctor,' Anna said when she'd finished with her questions.

Her mum echoed her words by saying now, 'Yes. Thank you, doctor. And especially for saving my life.'

He smiled at her now and said, 'Just doing my job, Mrs Sixsmith. If that's everything then, I need to go and continue my ward round.' He looked enquiringly at Anna but she shook her head and said, 'No, I think that's everything for now.'

'All right. Goodbye for now. I'll be visiting you every day, Mrs Sixsmith.'

'Thank you, doctor,' her mother said again and he left the room.

Anna exhaled and said, 'Well, at least now, Mum, we have some idea of when you'll be able to come home.'

'Yes, that's true,' her mother replied. Anna noticed her face had recovered some of its colour, which was good.

Gemma, who'd been standing quietly to one side throughout the whole exchange with the doctor, now spoke up. 'You'll be meeting your physiotherapist later on this morning, Pauline. You'll have to work hard with her but now I think it's time for you to rest.'

'Yes, I feel tired again,' she said and closed her eyes. So Anna just kissed her on the cheek and left with Gemma. Outside Anna said, 'It's been a lot for her to take in.'

'I know,' Gemma replied. 'But Mr Penny's very good at his job. He broke the news to her as gently as he could and he pointed out that the paralysis didn't extend to her face or her mental faculties, only to her arm and leg, so she's been very lucky in that respect.'

Silently Anna agreed, thinking how awful it'd be if her Mum's face was paralysed too or, even worse, if her mind was impaired.

Gemma continued, 'The Social Services will need access to your house to see what has to be adapted to your mum's new needs. Probably you'll need to have a stairlift installed. But they're rather slow and that probably won't happen for a couple of weeks. I'll ask Mr Penny to put a red flag on her file. That should speed things up a bit.'

'Thanks a lot, Gemma,' Anna replied.

'You go on home now and try not to worry.'

So Anna went back outside and got the bike. She cycled slowly home, thinking about everything Mr Penny had said. When she arrived, there was no sign of Peter and she presumed he was working. She knew she had to take her mind off the problems and decided to get down to her schoolwork. She did this for an hour or two, not very successfully she admitted ruefully to herself, and then went down to Peter's office and knocked timidly. When she was asked to come in, she went in and found him sitting at his desk surrounded by the usual apparent chaos.

He looked up from his work and said, 'Hi, Anna. So how did it go this morning?' And she told him. It felt good to be able to talk to somebody. Peter listened without interrupting and then said, 'Well, at least things are moving in the right direction.' And Anna knew he was right. She asked him if he wanted some lunch and he looked at his watch and said, 'Is it that time already? So it is. Yes, I'd love some lunch.'

So they went into the kitchen and prepared the food together. They ate in companionable silence and, when they'd finished, Peter asked, 'Do you think that maybe it's time to consider the possibility of going back to school? It's going to be rather boring for you around here otherwise.'

Anna hesitated and then said, 'Yes, maybe. But I'll still want to go in and see Mum every day.'

'You could do that after school, couldn't you?'

'Yes, I suppose so. I'll ring them up and see what they think.'

'Good girl.' And Peter left to return to his office.

After tidying the kitchen, Anna went back upstairs and rang her school. Classes were going on but, as soon as she announced her name, she was put straight through to the Principal who said, 'We've all been worried about you and your mum, Anna.'

'Thank you, Mr Docherty,' she said and she gave him the latest news of her mother.

'Well, I suppose it could be a lot worse,' he commented.

'Yes, indeed. I'm thinking now of coming back to school soon. Will that be OK?'

'Of course. You can start again tomorrow if you like. I'll inform your Head of Year and your form Tutor.'

Anna hesitated for a moment, wondering whether the next day was too soon, but decided that she might as well start then. 'OK. I'll be in tomorrow,' she said and hung up. She thought about it for a short while but she knew that the routine of school was exactly what she needed and she silently blessed Peter for suggesting it.

Then she decided to go back to the hospital to tell her mother about her decision. She wanted to ask her also about her appointment with the physiotherapist. So she pedalled slowly there and went, without rushing this time, up to her mother's ward. She at once saw Gemma who broke off her conversation with a nurse and came towards her. 'You're back, Anna!' she exclaimed. 'What brings you here now?'

Anna explained about her decision earlier and Gemma said 'Yes, I think that's a very good idea.' Anna then asked about the physiotherapist.

'Well, it was only her first visit of course but she told me that your mum was a fighter which is always a good sign.'

'Can I go in and see her now?'

'She was sleeping earlier but she may be awake now,' Gemma said and together they walked down the corridor to her room. When Anna peered through the window, she saw her mother lying peacefully in bed with her eyes closed. She asked Gemma about the feeding situation and was told that her mum had managed to have a reasonable amount of soup for lunch so they'd be taking out the drip later that afternoon.

'Good,' Anna said and went in while Gemma went back to her duties. She sat by her mother's bed and just watched her sleeping, thinking how much more normal she looked without the mask over her face. It must have been about half an hour later when she saw her mother's left hand twitch and she opened her eyes. She saw Anna immediately and said, 'It's you, Anna! How nice!' But then she burst into tears.

Anna had no idea what was wrong and just hugged her mother until the tears stopped. She had rarely seen her mum cry and was, in fact, rather embarrassed by her tears. She simply hadn't considered the idea that maybe her mum had emotions too about everything that had happened.

'I'm so sorry, darling,' he mum sniffled. 'I just couldn't help thinking when I saw you about all the trouble I'm causing you.'

'Don't be ridiculous, Mum! It's you I'm worried about, not me!'

'I know, darling, but still.....' and there she stopped, still obviously distressed.

'Please try not to worry about me. I told you I'm fine,' Anna said and then she continued practically, 'I came back, Mum, because I have some news. I've decided to go back to school from tomorrow so that means I won't be able to come in to see you in the mornings any more as I've been doing. But I promise to come every afternoon after school.'

Her mother seemed to cheer up at her words. 'That is very good, Anna. I'm pleased,' she said.

'How did it go with the physiotherapist?' Anna asked now, worried still about another outbreak of tears, but her mother seemed to have herself under control now.

'I think she's a closet sadist but she seems to know what she's doing. She gave me a list of exercises I have to do every day and made me promise to do them.'

'Gemma told me she said you were a fighter.'

'Yes, she said the same thing to me. I told her I've had to fight all my life. Do you see that yellow ball on my table? It's a stress ball and I have to keep trying to squeeze it as often as possible. But I keep dropping it and I get so frustrated.'

Anna passed her the ball and she took it with her left hand and put it in her right. She started trying to squeeze it and Anna could see the tremendous effort she was making but she could also see no movement in her right hand. It made her sad but she simply said, 'You just have to keep trying, Mum.'

'I know, child, and I will. I'm determined to beat this thing.'

'That's the spirit, Mum. Gemma just told me that they're taking out your feeding drip later this afternoon. Another step in the right direction.'

'Yes. At least I won't have quite so many wires leading into me. I'll be so happy when they're all gone.'

'So will I.' Then Anna had an idea and asked, 'Would you like to speak to anybody on the phone now?'

'I think I'm ready to speak to people. Could you ring Serena and Miriam and see if they're there?'

Anna already had their numbers keyed into her mobile and she dialled Serena's number first. She picked up almost immediately and Anna told her who she was and said her mum would like to have a word with her.

'Is she awake?' Serena asked excitedly.

'Indeed she is,' Anna replied and passed the phone to her mother.

They had a long and excited conversation which Anna tuned out and, when her Mum had finally rung off, she said, 'That was lovely. It's so good to be in contact with the world again. She said she'd come tomorrow afternoon and bring grapes *and* flowers to welcome me back. Could you try Miriam now? I know you'll probably get her answer phone but I should be able to leave her a message.'

Anna did so and did, indeed, get her answer phone. She passed the phone again to her Mum who left a long message. Then she gave the mobile back to Anna and said, 'I must get the phone in here fixed up soon. But I'll need some feeling in my hand first.'

'I'll do it whenever you want, Mum.'

'Thank you, darling. All this talking has made me sleepy again. I think I'll have a little nap now. You run along and I'll see you tomorrow.' With those words she closed her eyes and was soon breathing regularly and deeply. Anna sat and watched her for a while longer, then got up and left the room quietly.

She didn't see Gemma as she was leaving and went straight back down in the lift and outside where she took a couple of deep breaths, inhaling the warm air. It was another sunny day and she felt everything was going as well as could be expected. It was only then that she thought seriously about her mother's former tears and realised with shock that she'd been so wrapped up in herself she hadn't even considered her mum's reactions to everything. That made her feel very guilty and she almost ran back inside to apologise. But she finally, after some thought, decided it was better to leave well alone although she also decided that from then on she'd always put her mum first, not herself.

When she got home, she had tea and waited for Graham

to come back. He appeared at his usual time and they chatted for a while, Anna telling him most of her news but omitting her mum's tears, and then he excused himself to go and get changed and do his homework. Anna went for a stroll around the back garden and then impulsively decided to do something for herself for a change. She'd go to a movie.

She checked what was on at the local cinema on her laptop, noting the times of a film she thought might be fun, got some money out of the envelope and, after leaving Gemma a note to say roughly what time she expected to be back, cycled quickly to the cinema. The film was just about to start as she got there and she went in and lost herself for a couple of hours in the mayhem of a mindless futuristic thriller. As she cycled home again, she thought that the film was exactly what she'd needed.

Gemma was just about to serve dinner as Anna came in and she explained that she'd waited until the time Anna had put in her note to start. Anna thanked her and sat down with the family. Graham asked her about the film and she told him a little about it, emphasising that she didn't think it was his kind of thing. He grinned at this saying, 'Yes, you're probably right. But I'm glad you seem to have enjoyed it.' And she warmed to him all over again.

After supper she watched TV with Gemma for a bit but when the news came on, she excused herself, saying that she'd have to get up early tomorrow for school, and went to bed.

Chapter 18

She'd set her alarm clock for 6.45 and, when it went off, she got out of bed and went into the bathroom. There she had a quick shower, came out and got dressed in her school uniform. She checked herself in the mirror and thought she'd pass muster at school. She reckoned her classmates would wonder about how her spots had disappeared and might even ask her about it but she wouldn't have an answer.

Going downstairs she met Graham in the kitchen eating breakfast but there was no sign of Peter. She said 'Hi' and he responded briefly. After making and eating a quick breakfast for herself, she said. 'Bye' to Graham, who was still eating, and he responded by grunting. Then she went back to her room, got her rucksack and made sure she had all the school stuff she'd need. She put her mobile phone in although she knew she wouldn't be able to use it while in class, tidied her room and returned downstairs and outside to the bike. She found Graham had already left for his school and she pedalled away from the house, thinking not about her mother for a change but about the school day ahead.

When she arrived, she looked at her watch and saw it was 8.30. Good timing, she thought. She locked the bike in the bike shed and went in. There she found the usual pandemonium with everybody rushing this way and that to their classes. Rather diffidently, she went into her own classroom where she found many of her classmates already sitting at their desks and chatting to each other. They looked up as she came in and there was a collective rush towards her until she was surrounded by them, all asking questions. She answered a few but then her form Tutor came in and saw Anna. He smiled at her and said, 'Welcome back.' 'Thank you, sir,' she replied. Next the register was taken and the school day proper began. At break time she was surrounded by her classmates again and had to answer many more questions. One of them, a girl called Amy, who she actually liked, commented that she was looking good and Anna said, 'Thanks. So are you.'

The day passed inexorably and, when the final bell rang, she realised she'd slipped back into the routine as if she'd never been away. Everybody had been nice to her, which made a pleasant change, and she'd felt the sympathy from her teachers and the pity from her classmates. She got her bike and cycled slowly to the hospital, thinking how she'd tell her mother about the school day. When she got there, she went up to the ward and along to her mum's room without seeing Gemma. Her mother looked no different except that the feeding tube had now been disconnected, still with the white turban covering her head, and she was listening again to the radio. She smiled brightly when she saw Anna and said, 'Hello, darling! How lovely to see you! I've been a busy bee today.'

'Tell me about it, Mum,' Anna said, praying that she wouldn't burst into tears again like she had the day before.

But that Tuesday she seemed genuinely happy and said,

'I was with the physiotherapist for longer this morning and she says I'm doing well although I can't feel any difference yet. Then after lunch both Serena and Miriam turned up but not together and we had a lovely chat. In fact Miriam's just left. They both brought flowers.' Anna looked at the window sill where there were indeed two big bunches of flowers arranged in vases, which she guessed must've been provided by the hospital. 'But listen to me prattling on. Do tell me about your school day, darling.'

So Anna told her about the subjects she'd studied and how exceptionally nice everybody had been to her. Then she said with some trepidation, remembering how much her mum used to be against her cycling around the city, that she had borrowed a bike from Gemma and was now using it to get around.

But her mother just murmured, 'Well, you're a big girl now.' As she said this, Anna noticed her mother's eyes beginning to droop and she said, 'You must be tired, Mum. Why don't you sleep now?'

'Yes, I think I'll do that,' her mother mumbled. 'Thanks for coming in, darling. I'll see you again tomorrow.'

Anna waited until her breathing had become regular and she saw on the brain monitor that she was indeed asleep. Then she kissed her and left the room. She met Gemma in the corridor and asked if there was any improvement in her condition but was told that it was too early to expect any. She'd just have to be patient. As if she hadn't heard that before! Then Gemma smiled at her and said, 'I'll be back by 6.30. OK?' and Anna said she'd be expecting her.

She cycled home and got there just as Graham was arriving

too. They chatted about their respective school days while they had tea. Then they both went upstairs to change and do their homework. Anna found she could concentrate much better that day and it didn't take her long. After that she read for a while until 6.30 when Gemma came home and they prepared supper together.

While they were doing that, Anna asked her a professional question which had been bothering her for a while. 'How was it possible for my mum not to have noticed that she couldn't move her arm or leg until Mr Penny pointed it out to her?'

Gemma replied, 'It's perfectly possible to have the sensation of feeling in a limb even if you don't have it or it's paralysed. It's like those amputees who feel they still have limbs. Most people call them 'phantom' limbs. Have you heard of that phenomenon?'

Frowning, Anna said, 'No, I don't think so.' But she was satisfied with the answer and they dropped the subject, turning to Anna's school day which she told Gemma about, making her laugh a couple of times when she described the antics of some of her classmates. The rest of the day passed as usual and Anna went to bed, tired but satisfied.

She quickly found that she had indeed got back into the routine of school, with the addition of hospital visits of course, and the rest of the week passed uneventfully until the Saturday morning when she went to visit her mother. In hospital she was greeted by her with an ecstatic 'Hi, Anna! Look what I can do!' and Anna watched as she gave the little finger on her right hand a twitch.

'That's fantastic, Mum! I'm so pleased!' Anna said in delight.

'So am I,' said her mother. 'The physiotherapist was very happy with me. She says I've turned a corner. I feel I'm making real progress at last!'

'I knew you could do it!' Anna exclaimed.

'I'm not going to be stuck in this bed for ever,' her mother said with grim determination.

'Of course you're not.'

When Anna left the hospital after managing to talk to a doctor, she felt light-hearted, knowing her Mum should regain most of the feeling in her arm, if not all of it. Her leg was another matter. But they'd cross that bridge when they came to it.

The next day when she visited she was astonished to see that the brain monitoring machine was no longer attached to her mum's head and had been removed. She asked her about it.

'The doctors felt I no longer needed it,' she said. Anna had got so used to seeing her mother hooked up to the screen with the wires trailing from under the white bandage around her head that she thought she looked almost naked without them. But she was pleased again. It was another sign of progress. And over the next few weeks her mother continued to improve until at last she could flex all the fingers on her right hand and even raise her whole arm an inch or two off the bed.

Other things happened during this period too. The Social Services came round to the house after making an appointment with Anna, a man and a woman, and proceeded to go all over it, inspecting everything. Anna had taken the afternoon off school to let them in and watched as they tut-tutted, seeming to disapprove of almost everything they saw. But, when they came to leave, the woman said to Anna, 'Well, there's not much wrong with the house. But your mother will need a stairlift installed. Apart from that and a few alterations to the bathroom, the only things we would recommend are a number of cooking gadgets to help her in the kitchen. We'll get right onto the people who'll do the big jobs as soon as we get back and we can bring the gadgets over on Saturday if that's convenient for you.'

'Yes, that'll be fine. Thank you very much,' Anna said, relieved that they wouldn't have to demolish the house completely and rebuild it and blessing the NHS silently for their efficiency.

A couple of weeks later some men came round and installed the stairlift. It didn't take as long as she'd expected and, after it was done, Anna took a ride on it up and down the stairs. It was very easy to work and she was most impressed. On the same day a plumber came round and made the alterations to the bathroom, mainly, it seemed, making the shower easier to turn on and off which had always been rather hard to do. It all meant another day off school but Anna didn't mind. When the men finally left, she cycled straight over to the hospital to tell her mother the news.

'I'm not sure if I can take much more good news,' she joked when Anna had told her.

'It means that the day of your leaving this place is coming closer.'

'I know. I hope I'll be able to cope.'

'Don't forget. You'll have somebody to help you,' Anna said.

Her mother replied anxiously now, 'I do hope we'll get on.'

'I'm sure everything will be fine,' Anna said although she too had been worried in case her Mum didn't like the person allocated to her.

CHAPTER 19

And what of her relationship with Graham all this time? She continued to see as much of him as she could, especially at the weekends when they would sit for hours in his room listening to jazz and playing with his train set. He continued to treat her like a sister but occasionally, when he thought she wasn't looking, she caught a glint in his eyes and she knew that he fancied her. But she did nothing to encourage this, remembering her vow that nothing would happen while they lived under the same roof. He finished his GCSE's and the summer holidays were fast approaching.

They did, however, have one major argument during this period, which Anna found very distressing. She'd been thinking a lot about his privileged life style and she decided she just had to confront him about it. So, one day when they were in his room listening to music, she suddenly asked, 'How does it feel to know you have no money worries and will probably have none for the rest of your life?'

Graham looked at her goggle-eyed for a second and then said, 'What on earth prompted that?'

'I've been thinking about your school a lot and how lucky you are to be able to go there and get a decent education. You know you'll be able to go to a good university and get a good job later. But 95 per cent of the population aren't so fortunate. Most of them won't be able to afford to go to university, even if they were accepted, and so will be condemned to a life like their parents have – living on a council estate and all the rest of it.'

Graham listened to all this in silence but then he burst out, 'Aren't you a bit behind the times, Anna? England is a meritocracy now. Scholarships are available for people who can't afford to go to university.' He paused and then finished sulkily, 'And anyway it's not my fault if Peter knows how to make money.'

'I was hoping you wouldn't say that!' Anna retorted. And then she asked, 'Haven't you ever wondered how the other half live?'

'No, not really. I reckon that mostly it's their own fault. Look at how many benefit cheats there are. If they got off their arses and found a job, they'd be a lot better off than they are now.'

'Oh, you sound just like one of those dreadful Tory MP's!' Anna said angrily. 'Don't you see that social deprivation is at the root of most of the problems in England today? There's still an enormous gulf between the rich and the poor and it seems to be getting wider!'

'Well, what do you want *me* to do about it?'

'You could always do some voluntary work in one of the poor areas of the city! That might open your eyes!'

'But I'm too busy!' Graham wailed.

'Oh, you're useless!' Anna said furiously and stormed out. Later she felt sorry she'd given him such a hard time but not *very* sorry. She felt he'd deserved it. She did, however, promise herself never to discuss politics again with him.

They didn't talk for several days after this row and it was only when Graham came to her and told her that he'd thought seriously about what she'd said and would certainly consider the idea of doing some voluntary work during the school holidays that she partially forgave him. But it was not to be for quite a while until their relationship returned to its former even keel. And this only happened after they had managed to discuss the issues rationally, not in the heat of the moment. Graham apologised to her for his extreme views but told her that they were not really his, just things he'd picked up at school, and Anna managed to apologise to him for losing her rag. Peter and Gemma must've noticed the coolness between them but didn't interfere, leaving them to sort it out by themselves.

So, this major setback apart, everything appeared to be going well for Anna and her mother. Her Mum's hand and arm continued to grow stronger. Her own zits had completely gone now and so had her paleness. All her original colour had come back to her cheeks and she felt her confidence continue to grow. So things were getting better all the time. But this was not to last.

CHAPTER 20

It was a normal Monday at school and, after it was over, Anna set off for the hospital as usual. When she got there, she found the ward almost empty except for a nurse typing something up on a computer at the main desk.

'Where is everybody?' she asked the nurse who she knew.

'Hello, Anna,' the nurse replied in a sombre tone. 'Gemma's around somewhere. She's been expecting you and will explain everything.'

Anna ran down to her mother's room, worried now, but it was empty. She started to panic and called out urgently, 'Gemma, where are you?'

At that moment Gemma came out from a side room, wearing a mask. Slipping it off, she said, 'Oh, there you are. I would have called you but I knew you were in school and I decided to wait until you arrived.' Anna waited impatiently for her to go on and she continued, 'I'm afraid we've had an outbreak of MRSA on the ward. Most of the patients have been moved to the isolation unit as a precaution and the rest to other wards. I'm terribly sorry but your mum was one of the first to contract it. We're having to deep clean the ward now.'

Anna took a moment to assimilate this, then wailed, 'What *is* MRSA?'

'It's a rather virulent bug that happens occasionally in places like hospitals, especially big ones like this. Unfortunately, it's hard to treat with the usual antibiotics. But your mum's strong and she should be fine.' But her eyes were doubtful.

'Should be?' Anna cried. 'But will she?'

'I'm afraid only God knows the answer to that,' Gemma replied sadly. 'Come and sit down.'

But Anna didn't want to sit down. She wanted to hit somebody or something. Panic-stricken, she asked, 'Can I see her?'

'No, I'm afraid not. The precautions needed to enter the isolation unit are very stringent.'

Anna thought about this and then asked in a whisper, 'And if I'm willing to do whatever it takes?'

'I'm really sorry, Anna. But the answer, I'm afraid, is no.'

Anna's shoulders slumped in defeat and she felt like she might faint. 'But how could his happen? She was getting ready to come home!'

'I know,' Gemma said gently, putting an arm around her and supporting her to a couple of nearby chairs.

They sat down and weakly Anna said, 'After all her hard work, why did this have to happen to *her*?'

'It's not only her who's been affected,' Gemma reminded her.

Anna thought about this and then asked, her voice breaking, 'Could Mum die?'

'That's very unlikely, Anna,' Gemma said softly.

'But it *is* possible?' Anna persisted.

'Anything's possible,' Gemma replied. 'Oh, by the way, is your mum religious?'

This question seemed to come out of the blue but Anna

answered anyway, 'No, not really. She never goes to church.' Then she suddenly understood the reason for it. Gemma must be asking her whether her mum might need the last rites! What a truly dreadful thought!

But Gemma didn't explain why she'd asked the question. She just said, 'Now I think the best thing you can do is go home and wait for me. I should have more news by the time I get back although that won't be until later tonight. I already rang Peter and told him that. He said he'd prepare supper for you and Graham.'

'OK,' Anna said wearily and she pushed herself up from the chair. 'I'll wait for you.'

'Good girl. I'll see you later. Bye for now. Are you sure you'll be OK?'

'Yes. Bye,' Anna managed to say dejectedly. She walked to the bike and, her eyes blurry with tears, cycled home. On the way she only just managed to avoid colliding with a couple of cars which hooted at her angrily.

When she got back, she went straight up to her room. She felt like howling but controlled herself and wondered if there was anything she could do to help her mother. She could pray, that was true, but the atmosphere in her lovely room didn't seem quite right. She looked into the mirror. All she could see was her own pale, blotchy, tear-stained face which disgusted her so she went into her bathroom and washed it thoroughly but it didn't look much better afterwards. She lay down on her bed and, strangely, she soon drifted off into sleep and was only woken by an insistent knocking on her door. It was Graham telling her that supper was ready. She assumed it was the shock of the news that had made her sleep.

'Coming!' she called out groggily and stood up, swaying slightly as if she was drunk. She went back into her bathroom and washed her face again and combed her hair. Then, without bothering to change out of her school uniform, she staggered downstairs to the kitchen where Peter was waiting to serve supper.

Graham was already sitting at the table. He looked at her with pity when she came in and asked, 'How do you feel, Anna?'

'Not too good frankly,' she said. 'I'm not very hungry. Sorry Peter.'

'That's OK,' Peter replied. 'Eat what you can.' And he put a bowl of Gemma's tempting soup in front of her. She realised they both must have heard the news about her mum. Very slowly she took a spoonful of the soup. Peter had warmed a baguette and cut it into slices and he put this onto the table now with the butter dish. Anna automatically took a slice and put some butter on it. Then she looked up and saw them both watching her, Graham with tenderness and Peter with a worried look on his face.

'Gemma will kill me if you don't eat,' he said and Anna replied with a tired smile.

She forced herself to down the soup and a couple of slices of the baguette and then pushed her chair back and said, 'I hope you guys won't mind if I go back to my room. Please call me when Gemma comes back.' Peter promised he would and she left the kitchen with Graham still looking at her. He didn't seem to have started eating himself and hadn't uttered a word since his original question.

Back in her room she lay down on her bed again but

this time didn't sleep. She just stared at the ceiling with no positive thoughts at all, just ones of impending catastrophe, wondering what she'd done to deserve this and what she had to look forward to. She lay like that until well after dark until finally somebody knocked on her door. She jumped up, hoping it was Gemma who had come back. Now she was eager for news. Any kind of news. Whether good or bad. She just wanted to know what was going on.

It was indeed Gemma and she came in now, still wearing her uniform and looking unusually tired in the light from the corridor outside. Anna started to understand properly for the first time the stresses of her job. She turned on her bedside light and Gemma sat on her bed, taking her hand and smiling broadly.

'Good news!' she said. 'They've analysed the strain of MRSA and it's a common one. Hopefully, it'll be treatable with the drugs we have.'

Anna's heart leapt at her words and she said, 'When will you know for sure?'

'Not long. A couple of days at most.'

'If Mum survives this bug, how long will it take her to get better from it?'

'You're thinking about whether her return home will be delayed, aren't you?' Gemma said. Anna nodded and she continued, 'It shouldn't be delayed by more than about a week. Hopefully she should be almost back to where she was by Sunday.'

'Can I see her soon?' Anna asked now.

'Not until she's out of the isolation unit. But it should

only be a few days. Remember, though, she's not out of the woods yet.'

'I know that. But at least I've got *some* hope now,' Anna said. Then she put her arms around Gemma and burst into tears. Gemma hugged her back and let her cry. When she had no more tears left inside her, Anna took her head off Gemma's shoulder where it'd been lying and said with a lopsided grin, 'I'm afraid I've made your uniform all wet.'

'Don't be ridiculous, girl,' Gemma said with a grin of her own. 'I've had much worse things than tears poured over me in the past.' And she took the big box of tissues from the bedside table and handed it to Anna, who blew her nose noisily and dried her eyes. Then, giving her another hug, Gemma stood up and said, 'I've got another early start tomorrow and need to get my beauty sleep. You need to go to bed too. Will you be OK?'

'Yes, I think I'll be fine now. It's amazing what a good cry can do, isn't it?' Gemma gave her another grin and nodded. Anna added, 'I won't bother coming to the hospital until you tell me I can.'

'You're a brave girl, Anna. Try to sleep now.' And she walked to the door and let herself out.

Anna was all wrung out after her display of emotion but she decided to have a shower before bed. So, undressing, she went into the bathroom and bathed quickly. Then she came out, got into her pyjamas and climbed wearily into bed. She fell asleep almost immediately and didn't wake up until the following morning at her usual time.

When she got up, she felt reasonably rested and looked at herself in the mirror. The bags under her eyes were almost invisible, the blotchy look had gone and, although she was still a bit pale, she looked a million times better than she had the previous night even though, inside, she still felt shocked and terrified.

She debated what to do. Should she go back to school? On balance, yes was the answer. She would go mad just mooning about the house and wouldn't be able to concentrate on anything there. She had to take her mind off things. So she dressed again in her school uniform and went downstairs to have breakfast.

There she met Graham who looked up while he was eating and said, 'So you've decided to go to school.' 'Yes,' she replied shortly and quickly prepared her own breakfast. Graham didn't say anything else except 'See you later' before he left for St Paul's.

Anna had decided she wouldn't tell anyone at her school about her mother's latest setback. It would just be too trying to have to deal with all that sympathy again. So she continued with her old routine except that at home she said very little to the family and was left alone.

This continued for the next couple of days until one evening Gemma came back from work and said excitedly to Anna, 'The drugs are working!' Anna almost burst into tears again but instead they just hugged one another. 'It won't be long now until your Mum's released back into the ward.'

'Good,' was all Anna could find to say.

And indeed she only had to wait until the Sunday of that week before Gemma rang and told her she could see her mum. She pedalled as fast as she could to the hospital and ran up to the ward, which was bustling with activity again. It was a working weekend for Gemma and she caught sight of her talking to Dr Venju. Gemma noticed her immediately and cut short her conversation with the doctor. 'Anna, hello!' she called out and hurried over. 'Your mum's miles better. She's been moved to a bay now with other patients to keep her company.' And she took Anna by the arm and led her to one of the big rooms which had about eight beds in it.

Anna spotted her mother at once and ran over to her. She was listening to the radio again and looked much like she had the last time Anna had seen her although she seemed to have lost even more weight. To Anna's eyes she looked like a skeleton, a victim of a concentration camp, and Anna almost stopped in shock. 'Oh, Mum!' she cried and gave her a hug. She got a weak hug back and then her mother took off the headphones and said, 'Hello, darling!'

'You gave me such a fright!' Anna complained. 'I've been so worried about you!'

'I'll try to make sure it doesn't happen again,' her mum said with a flash of her old humour.

'It'd better not. Otherwise I'm sure I'd break down completely,' Anna replied. 'Anyway, how do you feel?'

'A bit weak to be honest but the doctors have assured me I'll be fine. Do tell me your news. What have you been up to?'

'I went back to school but I couldn't concentrate very well. I was just too worried.'

They continued talking for a while until a nurse came round and started fussing with her mother, doing all the usual things. When she'd finished, she said, 'It's time for you to rest now, Mrs Sixsmith.'

'OK. I'll be off,' Anna said and gave her mother another hug. 'I'll be in to see you tomorrow.'

'Lovely, darling! Bye for now.'

And Anna left.

CHAPTER 21

Her mother continued to get stronger. She was putting on weight and looked much better. The doctors were all apparently pleased with her progress. Anna was reasonably content now and got seriously back into her school routine, wanting to end the year with top marks, and her relationship with Graham grew warmer again.

One evening while they were watching TV together, Gemma said out of the blue, 'Anna, I have something to ask you,' and Anna looked at her expectantly. 'Some time ago we arranged for the three of us to go on holiday to Thailand for a couple of weeks to celebrate Graham finishing his GCSE's. I'd have liked to ask you to accompany us but I know you want to stay close to your mother, especially as the time of her leaving the hospital's approaching.' And here she paused but then continued, 'Peter and I were wondering if you might like to stay here while we're away and house sit for us. I'd show you how everything worked of course.'

Anna was dumbfounded at this suggestion and struggled to find words. She finally said, 'I'd be honoured to house sit for you if you're sure you trust me.'

Gemma smiled at her and said, 'Of course we trust you,

Anna. Otherwise I wouldn't have suggested it.' And so it was settled.

The day of their departure came and Anna waved them off in the taxi which was taking them to the airport. Peter's last words to her, said jokingly, were, 'No wild parties, please.' Gemma had already shown Anna how everything worked in the house, especially the washing machine, and had left her with a list of typed instructions. She'd also left the fridge and the freezer stocked up and given her the keys. She promised they'd ring as soon as they arrived. Graham was excited by the prospect of going to Asia as he'd never been outside Europe before. He'd done a lot of research on Thailand and even learnt a few words of Thai which he'd promised to inflict on his parents during the flight.

As Anna went back into the house alone, she wondered if she'd ever get to travel to distant countries but then put the thought aside as irrelevant to her present situation. She still had another couple of weeks of school before her own summer holidays started, Gemma having already explained to her that private schools had longer holidays than state schools. So at least she had her own routine to stick to while they were away and she didn't think she'd be lonely in the big house in the evenings or at the weekends.

Soon after they'd left, on another visit to the hospital, she found her mother with a lady she introduced as her physiotherapist. Her mum was out of bed and hobbling around, very slowly to be sure, on crutches. She was soon exhausted, however, and collapsed back onto the bed, breathing heavily. 'Pretty good, eh?' she panted to Anna.

'Absolutely bloody brilliant!' Anna said, smiling.

'We'll have her jumping around like a bunny rabbit in no time,' the physiotherapist said with a smile herself.

'Oh, I rather doubt that,' Anna's mother said but she also was smiling. Then to Anna she said, 'We had to wait until I had enough strength in my arm before I could use crutches.'

The next thing to happen was when her mother was introduced to her future carer, a professional nurse. Anna went into her room to find them in animated conversation. She was about the same age as her mother and it turned out that their interests were pretty similar. They seemed to get on well and Anna was relieved not to have to face another problem over that.

Her friends had been visiting her frequently and almost every time now Anna went into her room, she seemed to find another of them sitting by her bed. They all kept her amused and intellectually active which Anna knew was a good thing at this stage in her treatment. She was sleeping less these days and was positively bright-eyed and bushy-tailed most of the times Anna saw her. Both of them were finding it hard to contain their impatience over her going home and they both asked the doctors every day when it would be but they always received the same reply, 'Not just yet.'

But then one day Anna went in and found her mother in a state of high excitement. 'I saw Mr Penny this morning,' she said, 'and he told me I should be able to go home by the end of the week!'

Gemma and the rest of the family were now due back the next day and Anna knew that the timing couldn't be better. 'Fantastic!' she said.

'He told me that I'd have to keep coming to the hospital

every day for a while to see the physiotherapist but I don't care about that. I just want to be able to sleep in my own bed and have my own things around me.'

'I know you do, Mum,' Anna said gently.

'You've been wonderful, darling!' her mother said now. 'Come here and give me a hug!' And Anna did so, surprised by the strength in her mother's right arm. It was the first time she'd hugged her since the MRSA incident.

The next day the family duly returned, all looking tanned and fit. Anna had already tidied the house a bit and cleaned the kitchen thoroughly. She hadn't been a bit lonely while they'd been away, always managing to keep herself busy. Graham told her excitedly about some of the things they'd done, especially about riding bareback on an elephant through the jungle. That seemed to be the experience he'd enjoyed the most. Anna, when she could get a word in edgeways, told them the news about her mother and Gemma expressed great pleasure but Graham seemed downcast. 'Are you sorry I'll be going home soon?' she asked him. 'What do you think?' he replied enigmatically but Anna knew he'd miss having her around.

Then the end of the week came and all the arrangements for her mother to leave hospital were put in place. In the morning Anna had said a warm goodbye to Graham, giving him a peck on the cheek which had surprised him and made him blush, and a friendly one to Peter. An ambulance had been booked to take her mum home after lunch on the Friday. Anna spent the morning in her own house stocking up on food and doing a quick clean to make it ready for her mum, helped by Serena and Miriam. They'd promised to stay until after her mother arrived to make sure she'd settled in all right. It was the last day of term at school and her teachers had willingly given her the day off.

Gemma took her to the hospital in her car with all her possessions as she was to ride back home with her mum in the ambulance. She hoped it would be the final time she'd have to go there. When she arrived in the ward, she was astonished to see that her mother's white turban had been removed and her hair had clearly been washed and artfully arranged so that it covered any signs of the scar on the side of her head. She was also dressed in one of her prettiest frocks and had what she'd always described to Anna as her 'party shoes' on her feet, which Anna had forgotten she'd brought from the house some time ago in anticipation of this day. Without any wires attached to her now, although she'd lost a lot of weight and still looked frail, she was radiant lying there on her bed and Anna told her so.

'Thank you, darling!' she said. 'I have all my discharge papers here. I feel like I'm being released from a very comfortable and warm prison. We just have to wait for the ambulance now.'

CHAPTER 22

They had to wait until 4 pm for the paramedics to turn up but, when they finally did, they came equipped with a wheelchair which Anna's mother managed, with the help of her crutches, to struggle into. They left the bay after her mum had said goodbye to everybody there and found Gemma talking to a small group of the young nurses. She broke off when she saw them and walked with them down the corridor, into the lift and out of the hospital. The ambulance was there waiting for them and the paramedics lowered a kind of lift at the back and wheeled Anna's mother onto it. Then they raised it again until it was at the same height as the inside of the ambulance. There they lifted her gently out of the wheelchair and strapped her onto a bed. There was a bench opposite for Anna to sit on but she asked the paramedics if they could wait for a couple of minutes while she fetched her stuff from Gemma's car. She and Gemma carried all her books and suitcase back to the ambulance and she said goodbye to Gemma who gave her a kiss and made her repeat her promise to come and see them soon. Gemma wished her mum all the best and at last they were ready to go.

Anna's mother gave a huge sigh of relief as they set off and Anna sympathised with her feelings, knowing how desperate she'd been to get home. The driver went carefully along the busy roads without the siren on and quite soon they arrived in their own street. Anna looked out of the window and saw to her astonishment that their house was bedecked with bunting and had a huge banner hanging from the upstairs window saying 'Welcome back!' That must be Serena's and Miriam's doing, she thought, but she didn't tell her Mum, wanting it to be a surprise. Then she became aware of a scrum of people all waiting outside the front door, many of them with cameras. There was even a TV truck parked a little way down the street. Who on earth had told the press about Mum's release, she thought. And why are they interested in her anyway?

The ambulance parked in front of the house and the paramedics came round the back and opened the doors. Almost immediately flashes from the cameras started to go off and, as soon as her Mum was outside and in her wheelchair, reporters clustered around her. They were all shouting questions at her which were variants of 'How do you feel about the people who did this to you? Can you forgive them?' and Anna realised that, even now, more than two months later, the bombing was still news in the city.

Her mother meanwhile was totally bewildered by all the attention and she shouted at Anna above the clamour, 'I can't talk to them now!' but Anna didn't reply. She was too busy fighting her way through the scrum to the front door, closely followed by the paramedics, one of whom was pushing the wheelchair while the other was carrying her mother's suitcase and crutches. They seemed to be used to situations like this and to understand her mum's reluctance to talk and they formed a protective screen around her.

Fortunately the crowd parted enough to let them through and, when they got there, the door was thrown open by a smiling Serena who ushered them inside. 'Sorry about all that, Pauline,' were her first words to her mum, followed by, 'But you see how famous you've become. I've no idea who tipped them off about your release but no harm done, eh?' Her mother smiled wanly at her but asked no questions. The paramedic who'd been carrying her mum's suitcase went back to the ambulance to fetch Anna's stuff while his partner just stood there in the hallway, protecting them from the reporters outside. It took him two journeys to bring everything in and then they left with the thanks of Anna and her mum.

Finally they could relax and Anna wheeled her through to the sitting room where quite a number of her friends were standing around quietly sipping glasses of what looked like champagne. Anna had known that a small party had been prepared for her mum's homecoming but she was surprised by the number of people there. There was a big cry of 'Welcome back!' as they entered and Anna's mother looked as if she might burst into tears with surprised happiness. She was stunned by the welcome and said to Serena, 'I never expected this!'

'It's the least we could have done', Serena replied. Then somebody came up and thrust a glass of the white fizzy stuff into her mum's hand. She said, 'Knock that back, old girl. I'm sure you could do with it.'

'Thanks, Rachel,' her mother replied. 'It's the first proper drink I've had for what seems like forever.' And she sipped at her drink while everybody crowded round her, congratulating her on her release from hospital.

The party went with a swing and it wasn't until almost 8 pm that the guests started to leave, having eaten most of the food which Serena and Miriam had prepared earlier. Anna noticed that her mum ate and drank sparingly, clearly not used to the amount of food or the alcohol. She had, however, a healthy, young girl's flush to her cheeks and Anna could see how gratified she was to see so many of her friends together.

Finally the house was quiet. Everything had been tidied up and the last guest had departed. Anna could see that her mother was very tired. 'Time for bed, don't you think, Mum?' she said and her mother agreed. So she wheeled herself to the stair lift and got into it. Anna showed her how it worked and she was carried slowly up the stairs like some Oriental princess. 'That's fun,' she said when she reached the top. Then with her crutches she hobbled to the bathroom and got ready for bed while Anna went into her own bedroom and lay down on the bed, thinking about the day and how, apart from the reporters, it'd all gone rather well.

Then her mother went to bed and Anna stayed with her until she was properly asleep as she'd done so many times before in the hospital. Finally she turned off her mum's bedside light and left her bedroom. She got ready for bed herself, knowing her Mum's carer would be in early the next morning and she wanted to get a good night's sleep before she had to let her in. But she didn't manage to do so. She was still worried about the future and tossed and turned all night. In addition, her own bed was unfamiliar to her now and she found it hard to sleep.

Chapter 23

The next morning Anna woke up early with the sheets all tangled around her and she looked blearily at her clock on the bedside table. 6.45 – exactly the time she'd always got up for school at the Frost's house. However, today was Saturday and she felt she deserved a lie-in. But she knew she wouldn't be able to sleep so she got up, got dressed and went downstairs. Slowly she carried the rest of her stuff up to the bedroom from the hall where it'd been lying since her return home. She re-arranged all her books on her bookshelves and unpacked the rest of her clothes and put them away. Then she went in to see her mother but she was still asleep. So she went back downstairs and made herself some breakfast. After that, she just pottered around until the doorbell rang. It was the carer, exactly on time.

She let her in and, before she forgot, gave her a spare key to the front door so she could come and go as she wished. The carer, whose name was Felicia, went upstairs to see her mum and soon Anna heard signs of activity up there. She made breakfast for both of them and they soon appeared, her mother looking well-groomed and smart in one of her business suits. She greeted Anna warmly and Anna smiled saying, 'Breakfast's up, you two.' They both thanked her and sat at the kitchen table. Felicia only had coffee as she'd already eaten but Anna was glad to see that her mother ate everything that was put in front of her.

'How did you sleep, Mum?' she asked while she was eating.

'Like a log,' she replied. 'It made such a nice change not to be woken every two hours by a nurse wanting to check your temperature and blood pressure.'

'I'll bet it did,' Anna said.

Then the carer showed her Mum the kitchen gadgets which had been delivered and she was delighted with them, saying how useful they'd be. One especially caught her fancy. It was an ingenious device to help with unscrewing the tops of jars and she tried it on a new jar of jam. It worked perfectly and she pronounced it ideal. She still didn't have the strength in her fingers or hand to enable her to do things like that unaided.

Felicia, who was due to pop in three times a day to check on Anna's mother, left after promising to be back at lunchtime and asking whether there was anything they needed from the shops. It was a dreary old day outside, wet and gloomy, but Anna didn't mind. She was quite happy to stay in all day with her mum. They went into the sitting room and Anna switched on the radio and put it on Radio 2. Her mother seemed quite happy to sit there listening to the chat and the music and Anna went to do some homework in her room. Before she started, however, she rang Gemma but got Peter instead. He asked how everything was going and she gave him the news about the reporters and the party. He promised to pass it all on and she hung up. Then she got down to her studies and stayed in her room for the rest of the morning.

When she came down, she found Felicia and her mum in the kitchen. 'As it's only my first day back,' her mum told her, winking at Felicia, 'I'm letting Felicia do all the work. But soon she's told me I'll be taking over myself.'

'I'm looking forward to some of your lovely food again, Mum,' Anna said and her mother kissed her. After lunch she spent the time reading and, in the evening, once Felicia had left, she and her mother watched TV together, sitting companionably on the sofa, just like the good old days, Anna thought wryly.

Sunday dawned fine and she decided to cycle over to see Graham – Gemma had let her keep the bike on indefinite loan and she'd left it at home on Friday – and, when she got there, she found Gemma in the kitchen. They hugged and chatted a little, mainly about her mother, and then she asked Gemma if Graham was upstairs. 'I presume so. I haven't seen him since breakfast,' she replied. Then she asked Anna if she could stay for lunch and Anna said, 'Just let me ring home.' She did so and asked her mum if it was OK for her to stay at the Frost's for lunch and her mother told her that of course it was all right. She would have Felicia coming in later anyway. So Anna said to Gemma, 'Yes, that's fine although I didn't come over to bum some of your scrumptious food.'

Gemma laughed and said, 'I know you didn't, silly. Now run along and find that useless boy of mine.'

Anna found him in his room tinkering with his by now almost complete computer at his desk. He jumped up and ran over to her. 'Great to see you,' he enthused and planted a kiss on her cheek. She was surprised but gave him one right back and they both looked at each other. Graham blushed and mumbled, 'Sorry about that,' but Anna waved away his apology and said it didn't matter. He put on some jazz and they sat on the floor listening to it, chatting until their old kidding relationship was re-established and Anna knew he felt secure again.

Then they were called down to eat and after lunch Anna cycled home, pleased she'd gone over. She'd promised Graham that she'd come over again the following weekend and he'd seemed happy.

The weeks and months passed. Anna's mother slowly got stronger with the help of the physiotherapist who she saw every weekday, being given a lift to the hospital in Felicia's car, until finally she only needed a stick to help her walk. She took the crutches back to the hospital and told Anna she was glad to be rid of them. Anna was a mature sixteen-year-old now and preparing for her GCSE's. Graham was well into his A level courses and enjoying them, at last being able to study just the subjects he wanted to. He'd even done some voluntary work in an inner-city soup kitchen during the holidays, Anna joining him there briefly. He told her the job had depressed him although he added that it'd certainly been a worthwhile, eye-opening experience. Anna's mother was also starting to do some work again since she had only intermittent hospital visits now and Felicia had left them with promises to keep in touch, as she was no longer needed.

They'd had the Frost family over to the house several times for dinner at weekends and they'd both been over there too. Anna was pleased that her mum got on so well with them. She obviously approved of Graham and that was important to her. She continued her tradition of going over to their house every weekend if she could and, although she still hadn't said a word to her mother about her feelings for Graham, in fact they burned as strongly as ever and at last she felt everything was in place for her to make her move on him.

Why now? She knew she'd been through a life-changing experience and had, in fact, been forced to grow up, no longer just living in the world of her imagination, of her books. There was also her former fundamental lack of confidence when she was around other people which often used to come out as arrogance but which she now seemed to have overcome. The evidence for this in her own eyes was that she'd been made captain of her own school swimming team, something which pleased her enormously. She was excited now by the possibilities of adulthood and she at last felt ready for it. So it seemed the right time to finally break the bonds of childhood.

Therefore, one weekend about a year after her mother had had her accident she made extra special preparations for her visit to the Frost's. First she went to the hairdresser and had her long hair trimmed and layered so that it made her look older. Then she put on her best casual clothes and a silver bracelet her mother had given to her. She even applied a little makeup and dabbed some perfume behind her ears, things which she never normally did. She looked in the mirror before she left and pronounced herself satisfied. If she was going to seduce Graham, she knew she'd have to look her best.

On the way over to the Frost's she panicked and thought, 'No, I can't do this,' but the feeling soon passed and she kept going. When she arrived, she met Peter who looked more closely than usual at her and said, 'You look nice today.' Anna thanked him and asked if Graham was upstairs. He said yes and she went slowly up to his room, composing herself. When she went in, Graham bounded over from what he'd been doing at his desk and then stopped short just in front of her.

'You look different,' he said, frowning.

'Do you like it?' she replied, twirling coquettishly on her toes so that he could view her new hair style from all angles.

He hesitated for a second, then said, 'Yes, I think I do.'

'Put on some Miles Davis,' she commanded and he leapt to do her bidding. She sat on his bed rather than on the floor as was their usual custom and he, rather reluctantly, followed her and sat next to her. For a while they just sat there listening to Miles' amazing trumpet work but then Anna laid her head on his shoulder. He stiffened for a moment but then relaxed.

After more time had elapsed, Anna said dreamily, 'Do you like me, Graham?'

He pulled away from her and looked her in the eyes. 'You know I do,' he said.

'Enough to kiss me?' she asked. She could see the yearning but also the terror in his eyes.

Hesitantly he replied, 'I'm....I'm not sure.'

'Why don't we try it?' she suggested and leaned even closer to him. His face was only inches away from hers now and he closed his eyes, clearly surrendering to the inevitable. She put her lips on his and Anna could feel the last of his resistance slipping away. She applied more pressure and he responded, not very enthusiastically at first. But soon they were kissing passionately, if rather inexpertly.

When they came up for air, Graham said, 'You're a witch. You do know that, Anna, don't you?'

'Mmm,' she replied softly. 'But it's nice, isn't it? It's how it should be.'

'Does this mean we're an item then?' he asked hesitantly as if unsure of the answer.

"Yes, I suppose it does,' she said, nuzzling herself into his shoulder.

'Good,' he said. 'It's taken long enough.'

And they resumed their kissing.

When she returned home after lunch, she was almost skipping with joy and her mother, who was sitting in the living room, must've noticed the ecstatic look on her face as she passed. 'Why are you such a happy bunny today?' she called out.

'Oh, no special reason,' Anna called back airily as she bounced up to her bedroom.

THE END

RICHARD SLOANE spent the first 20 years of his professional life roaming the world as a peripatetic English teacher but then came back to his birthplace, Cambridge in England, to continue teaching for many more years. However, he was finally forced to retire due to medical reasons and turned to his first serious love, writing. In the last twelve years he has published 17 novels for all age groups as well as one book of short stories for very young children although this is the only book he has written for teenagers.